Up On the Creek

by

Tom McGlone

This book is a work of fiction. Places, events, and situations in this story are purely fictional. Any resemblance to actual persons, living or dead, is coincidental.

© 2004 by Tom McGlone. All rights reserved.

First published by AuthorHouse 05/05/04

ISBN: 1-4184-5995-X (e-book)
ISBN: 1-4184-3540-6 (Paperback)

Printed in the United States of America
Bloomington, IN

This book is printed on acid free paper.

DEDICATION

I would like to dedicate this book to my wife, Joan, author of SEARCHING FOR LOVE, who was so helpful and insistent that I do these short stories. Below is one of her unpublished but most beautiful, stories of an experience we both had in the Spring of two thousand three, while hiking in the hills around Berea Kentucky.

Thank you, Joan.

SPRING ON THE MOUNTAIN

We went to the mountain this morning! The parking lot at Indian Fort Theater was empty when we drove in. As we stepped from the car, our eyes began to feast upon the colors of trees and wild flowers and our souls feasted upon the quiet and tranquility. Dogwood and redbud trees greeted us as we walked along the path leading to the deteriorating concession building, a sad reminder of what once had been a wonderful outdoor theater portraying Wilderness Road. Then we began our climb.

It isn't as easy as it was a few years ago and we no longer go to the top of East or West Pinnacle but there are still spectacular views from every level. We were surrounded not only by the flowering trees, but also by wild flowers, some that we could not name. There were clusters of blue-violet bouquets covering the ground. You needn't be a horticulturist to enjoy the variety of colors that cover the forest floor. Names would not change their beauty. Some we did recognize; the violets, the may apples, not yet in bloom, and even the lowly dandelions added their own colorful touch.

We reached a sturdy wooden bench made by a Boy Scout troop and placed precisely where the view was the most awesome. We looked down from the ridge into valleys green with bursting leaves. A woodpecker was busy off in the distance and other bird songs lulled us into complete relaxation. Small skittering noises could be heard in the leaves of years past. Gone were the concerns of mowing lawns, starting the washer or vacuuming the living room.

A recently made comment by a good friend, Dr. Wear, came to mind as we continued to gaze around us, "Isn't it marvelous that God gave us the ability to see in color?" How true! The sky added its touch in a soft baby blue hue with a few smoke-like clouds floating about. A plane was in the distance followed by its vapor trail.

Too soon it was time to start wending our way back, back to our busy, busy world. Once again we heard cars in the distance. A sound we had so easily shut out while up on the mountain. As we retraced our steps, a silent prayer came to my mind. " Thank you, God, for allowing us one more time to enjoy the beauty of your creation."

Joan McGlone

PRELUDE

A soft summer breeze had begun to blow across the schoolyard bringing promises of much needed rain to the little valley of McGlone Creek. The annual homecoming was in full swing and as the sky began to show its dark clouds, some of the people began to leave the festivities. A church service had been held this morning and there were almost one hundred fifty people attending the gala events of the day. Many had come back to visit old friends, to form new friendships, to share in stories of the old days when many of them were children and lived up on the Creek. Some were here for the first time and everyone enjoyed the huge amounts of food placed before them.

A very lovely lady, Mrs. Sheridan, had become deeply involved in a conversation with me and she told me she lived in the old home place just down the road. My grandfather had built the house during the year eighteen-hundred seventy. My father had been born there so I was very interested in the house. I told Mrs. Sheridan I remembered the old fireplace and the mantel where my uncle had kept a large clock and the old family Bible. She invited me to see the house and I gratefully accepted.

Mrs. Sheridan explained that the staircase to the loft had been removed and a closet had replaced the steps. I remembered a portable pump organ my uncle had up there and I used to pound on the keys until I was told to quiet down!

She said it was probably still up there since she had not removed it when they cleaned out the room. Showing me a new trap door to the loft, she said I could go up there to look around if I wished to.

Climbing through the trap door, a blast of hot air hit me and I was almost smothered. The roof was tin and the heat all gathered in the attic, or loft, as she called it. I was surprised that she had not had trouble with that amount of heat stored up there. Off in the corner, amidst cobwebs and dead flies, stood the decaying organ. As I pulled it away from the wall to be closer to the light, the back fell off and a musty valise stuffed in the back of the organ fell out.

When I opened it, I found some very old yellowed papers.

Mrs. Sheridan gave me the valise and that evening as I sat with Cousin Carl, we read some of the papers and began trying to put them together in some order, being careful not to tear any of the pages. The information they contained gave us insight into what life had been like so many years ago.

Later when I left, darkness had settled in. As I said goodbye to Carl, and walked to my car, the frogs were singing, the mosquitoes were buzzing, and bats were in the sky. Anxious to scan the papers further, I hurried home to read more of Grandpa Thomas's writings.   By expanding on these stories, I offer to you—UP ON THE CREEK.

TABLE OF CONTENTS

UP ON PUNKIN' RIDGE

Nature's display of autumn colors was in full swing. Farris and his cousin, Carl were walking down the road to Ott's General Merchandise store from their homes up on McGlone Creek. The treetops reached across the narrow dirt road, which ran along side the creek and the yellows and golds were particularly brilliant, mixed in with the occasional red. Together they put on quite a show. The year was drawing to a close and soon the cold storms of winter would come to the hills.

"Carl, you know this walk is like we're under a canopy of gold. The leaves are as brilliant this year as I've ever seen. That red maple over there is really brilliant this year. Dad planted that tree when I was a youngster and put in some more to please mother. She enjoyed walking along here and watching the redbud in the spring and always liked the coloring of the leaves in the fall. Your dad helped to dig the hole and I believe our dads also dug up the tree back in the woods and moved it here."

"I don't remember, Farris. Maybe that was before my time."

The two walked on along the road enjoying the views and remembering how they played together as young boys.

Most every Saturday, the families up on the Creek would come into the village to do shopping or to visit with friends. Many of the men would stop in at Ott's to talk about crops while the women looked around for items they needed, whether it was at

Ott's or some of the other stores. There was a post office, another grocery store, a sawmill, a livery stable, a dry goods store and a hardware store, and new in town, a small gas station to service the few automobiles, which were now appearing in the area. The year was nineteen thirty-eight and electricity had just come to the Creek and it was gossiped that the telephones would not be far behind.

It was a bit chilly as they walked along but the briskness of their walking kept them comfortable. They opened the door to Ott's store and a swish of cool air settled over the men sitting around the snapping fire in the potbellied stove. Two men were having a checker game and by process of elimination with the other men, a champion would be crowned. When they saw Farris come in, some moaned because it was well known that Farris was the best checker player in the village.

Mac, who was involved in thinking about his next move, glanced up, "Sorry, Farris. It's too late to enter."

They all laughed. Mac had been trying to beat Farris for a long time now. Carl walked over to Mac and said, "Mac, Farris told me on the way here that he was going to let you win a few games before he got involved. Said he didn't want to waste his time beating you so often."

"No problem," Mac replied. "I have a new system figured out so I know how to beat him."

Again, they laughed. Mac had been working on this new system for a long time but it never worked.

Mac, while a good player, was no match for Farris.

The game was soon over and sure enough, Mac was the proud winner. Farris told him, "You're the champ, Mac. I'm not in the mood for a game today. So go ahead, enjoy it while you can."

The other men had decided they did not want to play anymore today.

The men sat around the stove although it was beginning to be too warm for them, and talked over what they had been doing. Harold had the only cane field in the valley and he had completed his molasses making for the year. He told them about one of his boys tripping and falling in the molasses pans.

"He didn't get burned since the pan was just beginning to warm up but he did learn his lesson, I hope. He had been chasing that little Kiser girl around the mule's path and got himself tripped up in the harness. Serves him right but I'm glad he didn't get burned. Don't any of you ask; I did go ahead and use the molasses!" That brought another burst of laughter from the men and caused young Harold Jr. to run out of the store in embarrassment.

Carl said, "Harold, that's too bad but it's better than you getting your beard caught in the syrup." A few years ago, Harold had to have his beard cut off because he had tripped and his face fell in the new molasses. Harold Sr. turned a dark shade of red as the men laughed.

Everyone had their tobacco drying in the barns and most of the corn had been stored for the winter, so it was a comfortable time for the farmers. They could sit around and tell tales and laugh at each other with no offense taken. Some had brought persimmons and paw paws to Ott for him to sell, Harold had brought molasses and there were a few who had popping corn. Some of the women brought in quilts and a few pies. Ott would take these things to the nearby town and place them on sale and would share the profits with the farmers.

Ott opened the door of the stove to let the fire burn out since the day was beginning to warm up. The lingering smell of wood smoke and spice permeated the air.

The wind was picking up and outside one could see the leaves falling and there was a feeling of possible rain in the air. Some of the women had come in the store to tell the men folk that they were going to the schoolhouse to prepare for the pie supper that night. After the pie supper, there would be a movie shown on the new DeVry projector the school had purchased since the inception of electricity. This would be quite a night in the little village and it was not beyond reason that a few of the men had brought along some liquid refreshment!

The lingering talk quieted down and several men were just sitting around on nail kegs, or flour sacks and some were smoking pipes, others just sitting with an occasional comment. Carl suggested they have Farris tell them a story while waiting for the now present rain to end. Farris had been a schoolteacher in the village and everyone there knew and respected him.

Most all of the people in the valley had attended his classes since he was about the oldest resident there and had taught for most of thirty-five years. He often said he would still be teaching if it weren't for the corruptness of the present school system. Farris was approaching eighty years and was still sharp of mind and body. He would walk for miles, disdaining the use of the new automobiles or even wagons. Said walking was good for him!

They all wanted him to tell a story, a thing he had often done in the past, and they had enjoyed his tales. Farris asked Ott to pass around some of the caramel candies he kept in stock and told him to put it on his bill. Ott replied, "Farris, you've told me to put it on your bill every time you've been in here, but you haven't settled you bill with me yet." Passing around the candies, Ott knew the men all were aware that Farris paid cash for everything he purchased but they enjoyed kidding him.

Farris sat down on a nail keg, was quiet a moment, seemingly lost in thought, and then he spoke up.

"I was a lad of about eight or nine years of age and we lived in a two-story house up on the Creek, the one which is just across the bridge and is painted white now. My dad had been in the Civil War and when he came home, he and mother soon married and they wanted their own home as soon as he had time to build one. Before the war, he had been living in a small log cabin with his parents and being newly married, he and mother wanted to be by themselves. Soon, he was able to complete the house with the help of neighbors, and they moved in much to the delight of mother. They raised a large family and I was one of the youngest.

One Saturday afternoon the folks living on the Creek held a basket supper in the new school/church building which dad had built for use by the neighborhood. Mother, dad and I went, and when the party was over, and every one was gone, we stayed to clean up the building. Dad insisted the building be nice and clean for church services next morning. The visiting preacher came once a month and that Sunday would be his day.

After the work was done, mother and dad gathered up their things and we headed off for the mile walk home. Outside the building, there was a big, full moon hanging just over the hills and dad said we wouldn't need a lantern that night. I had run on ahead of them, and about half way home, I got plumb scared out of my wits! I looked over to the side of the road and there were some yellow eyes looking back at me. I thought at first it was fireflies, but then saw that it was probably a 'coon or possum. 'Dad,' I called, 'Come quick.'

Dad hurried up to me, looked at the little animals and said to me, 'Boy, I believe you've found some puppies. Leave them alone now. Their mother must be nearby so she'll take care of them.'

I remember saying to dad that they didn't look too good. I told him I would like to take them home and feed them. Dad looked a bit closer and said, 'Farris, I think you might be right. Maybe something happened to their mother. We'll just put them in the picnic basket and carry them home.'

Mother didn't particularly like the idea of him using her basket, but he gently picked them up, put them in the basket, and made me promise to feed them when we got home. Then I could put them on the back porch where their mother would probably find them later.

We hurried home. Mother went out to the kitchen to warm some milk so we could feed them with a bottle. Then, since dad tried to keep stray animals away from the house, he said we should take them out to the barn. He took down some horse blankets from the hayloft, and made them a bed.

Next morning, while we were doing chores, the visiting preacher arrived in a buggy ready for church services. Looking at the animals, he told dad he thought the pups we had picked up were wolf cubs, not dogs.

Dad told the preacher that no wolves had been seen here for at least fifty years. He agreed they didn't look like normal puppies but just couldn't believe they were wolf cubs. At the same time, dad wondered how they got here if they were indeed wolves.

The preacher thought about it and said, 'Thomas, I don't know how they got here but I really think they are wolves.'

We went off to church and as soon as the services were over, I hurried home and went to the barn to see how the little critters were doing. I played with them awhile and fed them some more warm milk. When dad and the preacher came to the barn, they agreed they might be wolves. Dad again said he didn't know how they got here in the valley, but we couldn't keep them around the house. He told me I could take care of them a bit longer, and then we would have to take them up into the hills and turn them loose.

The puppies, or wolf cubs, grew rapidly with our feeding them regularly. The biggest one was a male and I named him Nick; the other three were females and I didn't give them names. Nick always wanted to be with me and would growl at the others if they came too close. He was showing the others he was the leader of the four.

Telling me they were wild animals and needed to be free, dad said the time had come to take them into the hills. He had killed some rabbits for us to eat, and we took some of the leftovers with us as we walked up to one of the ridges surrounding the valley. When he turned the wolves loose, he left some of the rabbit meat nearby and they soon discovered it and quickly ate it all.

Dad told me we would have to leave them on the ridge. They would have to learn to hunt and there was plenty of small game and deer around so the cubs should be all right. He again explained to me that wolves are meant to live in the wild and not to be kept as pets. Dad walked back down the hill toward the house and called to me to come with him. He assured me they would be all right. When we walked around to the front of the house, our neighbor,

Marion, was sitting on the porch talking to mother. He had his shotgun and told us he was going to hunt some rabbits and wanted to know if dad would like to join him. I knew dad didn't like to kill wild animals except when we needed some to eat, so he turned Marion down. When Marion walked away, dad said to me that he was glad I didn't tell Marion about the wolves because he would try to track them down and kill them.

A few weeks passed and almost every day I went up on the ridge to see them. I would occasionally take them some meat we had left over from our butchering, and sometimes they were there and other times there was no sign of them. As time passed, I saw less and less of them, but whenever they saw me, they would lay down nearby and just watch me, but wouldn't allow me to get too close. It was as though we had developed a friendship together, but they were still wild animals. I guess a year passed and I still went up on the ridge most every day. Sometimes there would be signs they had been there but I rarely saw them.

Once, on a hot summer afternoon, I had been lying there on some soft moss looking up at the clouds and I guess I fell asleep. Suddenly, I felt something licking my hands and I jumped up; there was Nick sitting near my shoulder. The other three were just off by the edge of the clearing. I reached out to pet him but he backed off like he just wanted to say hello, but not for me to touch him. Dad had told me wild animals didn't like humans to touch them. Well, I sat there for a while and Nick and the others just lay down nearby and watched me and dozed a bit and together we shared what God had given us. There was a feeling of total peace and contentment. After awhile, Nick got up, looked at me, wagged his tail and walked off into the forest. The other three followed him, and as they got to the brush, they all stopped, looked back at me as if to say goodbye, and disappeared. "

*****

Ott brought some hot chocolate to the men, so they sat there sipping on the chocolate, and then one of the young boys who had come in the store in time to hear the story, spoke up, "Go on with the story. We want to know what happened."

Farris asked Ott for a grape soda, and after drinking it, he went on

"That evening, I was telling dad what had happened and he told me the wolves had probably moved to another area since the deer were scarce in the valley this year. There had been no lost cattle so dad wasn't worried about that. I watched for the wolves off and on for another year. At times I thought I could see signs they had been there, and one night I thought I heard them cry from up on the ridge.

One day I was walking up in the hills not far from the ridge, and I saw movement off in some brush and I knew it was Nick and his sisters. I hurried to the clearing and in a little while there they were! I sat under a big beech tree and they came up close to me and acted like they were glad to say hello again. They played a bit there in the clearing, and then lay down in the grass and kept their eyes on me. I was getting close to twelve years of age and was trying to help dad on the farm. I heard him calling me to come do my chores, so I had to leave the wolves there, and in my innocence, I said for them not to go away, that I would be back soon.

I ran to dad and said I had seen Nick and the others, and wanted to go back later to see them again. He said I could as soon as I finished the milking, so I hurried and when I was done, I ran all the way back to the ridge. They weren't there! I guess I had a tear or two as I called out to Nick but there was no sign of them. I stayed until after dark, then I had to go home.

That night we were out on the front porch and mother and dad were sitting in the swing, and we were watching the fireflies and listening to the far off cry of the whippoorwill. I told them about seeing the wolves and wondered if they might be coming back to stay. Dad lit up his pipe, came over to the steps and sat by me.

'Son,' as he put his arm around me, 'I doubt if they will ever be back. There are too many people living in the valley and wolves are afraid of people. Best you forget them. '

Dad got up, stretched his back and said it was bedtime. The full moon had come up over the hills surrounding the valley and Dad said this night reminded him of the time we found Nick and the others up the road. He ran his hands through my hair and said we should go to bed since we had a big day coming up tomorrow.

That night I lay in my bed with the window open to catch a cool breeze, but I couldn't sleep. I kept thinking of 'my' wolves and what they might be doing and where they were. As I tossed and turned, I heard in the quietness of the night, some shotgun shots and called out to dad that someone was out hunting. Dad called back to me that it was probably some 'coon hunter. He said he had heard the dogs a short time ago.

I was satisfied and I finally dropped off to sleep. Next day, I had finished my chores and was sitting in the barn watching dad work on some harness, when I decided to go up the ridge to see if there was any sign of the wolves. I really didn't expect to find any because I figured they had left the valley for good. I took my time, stopping at the creek to watch for some fish, and when I got to the clearing on the hill, I saw three animals lying there on the ground. I thought it might be the wolves returning so I walked slowly toward them so they wouldn't be scared. But they didn't move! As I got closer, I realized they were the wolves and they had been shot. I ran to them, put my arms around them and realized they were dead. I cried out and took off running to the house calling out for dad, and I remember tears were running down my face. He heard me coming and came running toward me. I told him what I had seen and he took me by the hand and we went back to the ridge. There they were, the three female wolves with shotgun pellets in them, killed the night before. Dad said we had best look for Nick because he might be hurt and would need us. We looked around but saw no sign of him, and I kept calling out to him, but he wasn't there.

Dad was very emotional and I know there was grief in his eyes. He said he would go back to the house and get a shovel, so we could bury the wolves. As he hurried off, he told me to stay there and look around to see if I could find Nick. When he came back, I was sitting there beside the three dead wolves with my arms around them. I know I was crying because dad told me to use my shirt to wipe my face.

I was still crying as we buried the three of them in the deep hole dad had dug. He put a few rocks on top of the grave so I could remember where it was. I kept looking off into the woods to see if I could locate Nick, and once I called to dad that I had seen him. When he looked up, he saw nothing and said he thought I was imagining things. To this day, I believe it was indeed Old Nick watching us bury his sisters.

Dad left after he put the rocks on the grave, but I stayed for a while looking for Nick, and occasionally calling out to him. I finally gave up and went home. When I got there, Marion, our neighbor was just leaving. Dad walked over to me and told me Marion had told him about being out 'coon hunting last night and had seen some large animals up in the clearing. He thought they might be deer so he shot them but when he looked, he saw they were dogs so he just left them there. I'll never forget dad saying that Marion should be shot just like he did the animals. I was shocked to hear my dad say such a thing because he never said anything like that before! I've always remembered dad teaching me never to mistreat any animal. He even hated to shoot rabbits and squirrels, and he would only shoot a deer if we needed some meat for food.

The next morning, Marion came riding up on his horse and told dad that some animal had attacked his 'coon hounds last night and had slashed their throats. He was upset and said he couldn't understand why any animal could do that without being hurt itself. As he rode off, I heard dad say that it served him right!

That night, we again were sitting on the front porch, and mother and dad tried to explain to me that things like that happened to wild animals when they got too close to man. Dad said it sometimes seems cruel and maybe we can't always understand why man has to kill, but he does.

I couldn't sleep that evening and sometime during the night, I heard some noise coming from down around the barn. The horses were restless and I called to dad. He was already up, and told me he had heard the noise. He was going to take a lantern to the barn to see what it was.

I got up with him and as we were about to leave the house, we heard the low, sad, mournful cry of a wolf. It was coming from under my window, or near my window. I hurried into the night calling out to Nick because I knew it was him. There was nothing there. No sound, no movement, just total stillness. A few minutes later, dad and I heard it again. From off in the distance up on the ridge, there came the wailing cry of a wolf, only this time it was loud and seemed even sadder. It sounded out over the valley again, and then it seemed a deep loneliness had settled in. Then-- nothing! Not a sound. For several minutes we heard nothing, and then the frogs began their calling again and that was all.

I looked at dad and said, 'That was Old Nick, wasn't it Dad?'

He placed his arm around me and told me that he believed it was. He said it was Old Nick coming to say goodbye to me. He held me while tears came to my eyes, and said he doubted if I would ever see the wolf again.

He thought Old Nick had said goodbye to me and then went up on the ridge to say goodbye to his sisters. I remember dad telling me how I had been blessed by having Old Nick as a friend.

Days passed and they grew into years. I grew up, taught school for several years, and then left the Creek for a period of time. I would go back for a visit occasionally and then one summer dad died and mother followed soon afterward. We buried them up in a little graveyard overlooking the schoolhouse. After that, I didn't go back for a long time.

One day, I received a letter from Mort, a cousin of mine, inviting me back to the Creek for a home coming celebration. My son took me, and that was the first time I had been up the valley for about twenty years. The celebration was held at the old school/ church building father had built, and after it was over, I was invited to Mort's home for a visit. We drove up the road toward his house and as we passed the cemetery, I got out of the car, and went to see mother and dad's graves. I stood there remembering the good times I had with my parents, but I suppose I was ashamed to show emotion in front of my son. I felt it though, I had it deep in my heart as I thought of mother and father, and the hard times they had gone through.

My son, Elton, and I had a good visit with Mort and his family, and it soon came time to leave. The goodbyes were said with promises to come back soon. As we walked outside, far off in the woods, we could hear the call of the whippoorwill. The night was filled with the light of fireflies and just over the hill, the moon was rising.

We rode down the road past the schoolhouse, and as we got close to the old home place, I asked Elton to stop the car. He did, and I got out and stood there in the moonlight-filled night with my thoughts.

A cloud moved over the moon and suddenly I heard it--the lonely, sad wail of a wolf. It was Old Nick calling to me from up on the ridge!

I asked Elton if he had heard that.

He said he hadn't heard anything other than the frogs singing.

As I stood there in the quietness of the night, a big lump came in my throat, a few tears rolled down my cheeks and I thought to myself, "No, I guess you wouldn't."

It was between Old Nick and me. For a minute we were together in memories, me and Old Nick up there together--up there on Punkin' Ridge."

*****

Farris took out his handkerchief, blew his nose. Quietness settled over the store. Some of the men sniffed, others wiped their eyes as though something was in them, and others got up and walked out into the deepening night.

GRANNY

"How is the most beautiful mother in the world?"

"Edward? Is that you? Where are you? What does a mother have to do to see you again?"

"I don't know, Mother. It has been a long time since I've talked with you! Almost two weeks! I guess you could invite this wayward son home to a breakfast of biscuits, gravy, eggs and sausage. What are you doing today?"

Looking quickly at her calendar, she held the phone close and replied, "Nothing at all. Don't tell me I'm going to be blessed with a visit from you? When can you be here?"

"I'm about a mile away and I want to talk with you if you have some time today. I have to go back to school tonight. My big test is on Friday and I still need to do some cramming. I want to talk with you but I need to do it when you're alone. I'll be there in a few minutes."

"I'll turn on the oven and start breakfast. 'Bye!"

Edward had been up most of the night driving down to see his mother. As he hung up his car phone, he smiled to himself. His life had been almost ideal. He had a wonderful mother and a stepfather who had given him much love. His two sisters, Michelle and Misty, were wonderful and both were now in college. He loved to visit with them, but today, he wanted to see his mother alone, and so he had left the campus late last night and had driven all night to see her. His step dad was away attending a conference on Ancient Bible Times and the two girls would not be home since they were also studying for exams, as he was. He was to get his Doctorate in Biblical Studies at the end of the month but he had to defend his thesis this coming week.

Parking in the driveway of his home, he waved to his mother as she stood in the doorway.

"Hi there, Mother."

"Edward! It's wonderful to see you. I certainly didn't expect you this week. I thought you had a lot of research to do and dad and I were expecting to help you celebrate at the end of the month."

"I really shouldn't be here right now. I'm loaded with work and I have to defend next week. I have something to talk with you about. Something, which has been bothering me for several nights now. I hope you don't mind me dropping in on you like this."

"Son, you know you can come home anytime. What's bothering you? Come on in the kitchen and we'll talk while I get the food ready."

"Oooohh. That sure smells good. Mom, you're the best cook there is. How very much I miss sitting here at the table while you cook up a big meal." Edward laughed as he hugged his mother and then he sat down to watch her work.

"You can't sit and watch, you know. You have to help out if you want to eat soon. Set the table and don't forget the napkins."

This had been a private joke between them for years. When Edward was growing up, he would use his shirtsleeve instead of a napkin, no matter how hard they tried to break him of his habit. As he got older, his sisters would tease him about not using a napkin and then they would all laugh about it.

Edward's mother had inherited quite a sum of money from her parents so his family had always lived comfortably, but not pretentious. His stepfather was the minister of a large church and well liked by the community in which they lived. Michelle and Misty had graduated with honors from high school and were now attending a college in Ohio, one a senior, and the other, a sophomore. Edward had always been the favorite with his mother, even though she tried hard not to show it. He had played ball in high school and also in college until his workload had become too heavy for him to combine sports and studies. He was only a fair student in his undergraduate work but when he decided he wanted to go on with his education, he dug down deep and became a scholar of the Bible, following in his stepfather's footsteps. He was top student in his class and was becoming well known in the School of Religion with his published papers and a book he had only recently had published. Several universities were waiting for him to finish with his doctoral work and then they would offer him a professorship in his field. He had not accepted any offer however, stating he was not sure how he wanted to use his knowledge.

His mother stirred the gravy, he set the table and soon the food was ready and a hungry man and his mother sat at the table. He was ready to 'devour' the food and laughingly, she patted him on the shoulder and told him to go ahead.

"Mom, I miss this most of all. Some day, if and when I get married, you must write down the recipe for all of this. Maybe I should test the lucky young woman to see if she knows how to cook!"

"Yes, you do that, and you might not have a wife after all! Not many women like to be told, 'That's not the way my mom does it.' You'll see and hopefully, learn, before it's too late. And how about that subject? Are there any young ladies in your immediate future? You're not here to tell me you're going to be married?"

Edward laughed as he mixed up the eggs and biscuits and covered them with gravy.

"No, Mom. I've been dating a girl for a while but there is nothing serious about it. I haven't had time this past year. I'm about through with my studies and until I am, there can be no distractions. One more week and I should have it wrapped up. My advisor tells me I have nothing to worry about."

"Good for you, honey. Now what do you want to talk with me about? Your father will be home this afternoon and he will be disappointed not to have seen you. Do you really have to go back so early?"

"I'd like to take a short nap later and then I really have to go. I have one more paper to complete and that's it. I should be back by the end of next week. Let's do the dishes and I'll talk as we work."

"No. We'll go in the den and talk and I'll do the dishes as you nap."

Sitting down in a big chair, Edward spoke quietly.

"For the past several nights, I've been having what I call dreams, about a strange woman. She is sitting on the porch of what looks like a farmhouse, in a rocker. She has a bonnet on her head and an apron tied around her waist. She is always smoking a corncob pipe.   When she talks to me, she shows she has no teeth and is always waving her arms like she wants me to come to her. She seems very old but very alert. At first, I thought nothing about this and had laughed with one of my professors about it as we talked over some studies I had done. But now, she is talking to me and I can understand most everything she says. Just two nights ago, she waved and said for me to come on home for a while, to visit my other family. I could hear her so plainly that I woke up and was perspiring. I believe I started the dreams about two weeks ago but it has been a constant thing for four nights now.

I know you have always been honest with me about my real father but when she said for me to come home for a while to my other family, I got to thinking about what she meant. Do you know anything about this old woman, who she might be, and what she might mean to me? Maybe if you tell me again about my father, it might help. Do you mind?"

"No, dear. Of course I don't mind. But it's been almost thirty years and I don't remember much. And no, I know nothing of what you're seen in your dreams."

Edward rose out of his chair, hugged his mother and said he was so fortunate to have her.

"I don't want to cause any problem for you but tell me again about you and my father. I need to know it all so I can figure out this woman in my dreams. It's beginning to bother me and I would like to solve it."

His mother paused a minute and then spoke,"Well, I had been in college and a girl friend had asked me to come visit her over a holiday. I don't remember which one. She lived in a small town in Kentucky and one night while I was there, we went to a pie supper they held at the local church. We baked pies and the men were supposed to bid on them. The man who bought your pie was supposed to eat dinner with you that night at the church.

Jenny had her boyfriend bid on her pie so she could eat with him. Unknown to me, another friend of hers bid on my pie and it had been arranged for him to be the highest bidder so he could eat with me.

After the dinner was over, the four of us went to Jenny's house and the man I was with, Essie, was a great story teller so he kept us amused most of the evening. Jenny and I were leaving for school next morning so we said an early goodnight to the men and went to bed. Next morning as we were getting ready to leave, Essie and Jerry stopped by to again say goodbye to us. Essie asked me if he could come see me at college and I hesitatingly said yes. We left and I wondered if I would ever see this man again. He was a charming person and seemed to be a very perfect gentleman. I suppose I was disappointed that he never called, and one day Jenny's boyfriend showed up and said that Essie had been drafted into the army sooner than expected and did not have a chance to tell me. He asked if Essie could come see me when he was home on leave and again, I hesitatingly said yes.

About two months later, Essie called and said he was home and wondered if I would see him. He was all apologetic about not contacting me before and I accepted his apologies. After all, we had just met once and there was no reason to think either of us had to apologize to the other.

I was a young woman of nineteen and when Essie arrived, I knew I was in love with him. Of course this was silly. We had really only been together for a short time and I knew nothing of him. He stayed in the area a week and then he had to go back to camp. We corresponded by mail and he called a few times. One day he called and said he would be home for three weeks before he had to go overseas and wondered if he could see me. As I told you, I felt I was in love with him, so this time I eagerly said yes.

He came to see me almost immediately and we saw each other every possible minute while he was here. He had to go home to visit with his parents and asked me if I would go along. Foolishly, I said I would go and when we arrived, his mother was very unhappy with him for not spending more time with them. And she wasn't too happy with him for bringing me home with him. We were with them for three days. One day, while walking out on his father's farmland, he asked me to marry him. He said we wouldn't have much time and he knew we didn't know each other very well but he would make it up to me when he got home. I agreed and when we broke the news to his parents, they were horrified, and so were mine when they heard about it. However, we were determined and a quick wedding was arranged and two days before he had to leave, we were married.

I decided I would go with him when he left and stay with him until it was time for him to leave for overseas. The day before his ship was due to sail, I was in our apartment busy packing to go home, and he said he was going to go to the store to get some milk and bread. I told him I would go along but he said he would only be a few minutes. The store was just a block away. He didn't come back so I began to worry about him. I started to go out looking for him when there was a knock on my door. Thinking it was Essie, I opened the door and there were two policemen standing there. They asked if they could come in and then they told me that my husband was struck by a car as he crossed the street and had been killed instantly. The driver of the car had been drinking, and he too, was killed in the wreck.

The man, Essie, was your father. I found out about a month later that I was pregnant and cried for days.

My parents were rather well to do and they took me in with them and gave me all I needed. I didn't have to work or to worry about anything but I suffered so much at the loss of your father that they became worried about me and had me see a doctor. I was in counseling for several months. By the time you arrived in this world, I was fine. You'll never know how much I loved you when you arrived and I still love you as much today."

"I know you do, Mom. I know. And you've shown it. And I love you also. I think I need to find out who this old woman of my dreams is and I thought you might be able to help me. I suspect she is someone of my father's family although I'll never know why I'm dreaming of her. I don't recall ever seeing any of his family."

"No, I don't think you ever did. His parents never really accepted me and they pretty much ignored me at his funeral. I never heard from them after your father was buried so I felt they didn't care. I always felt badly about that and back then I often felt I should make an effort to see them. I wrote them a letter after you were born telling them how lovely you were and I thought they might like to see you. They never replied and a few years later, I heard from my friend, Jenny, that they had both passed away. From that day on, I never heard anything about your father's family. Three years later, I met Donny; we got married and you know most of the rest. I wish I could help you but I don't know how."

"I wonder who this 'granny' is? I don't think there is any connection because I certainly don't know any of them. But I need to know about his family. Do you mind if I try to find them? If you do, I won't pursue it any further."

"No, of course I don't mind. I just had a thought. I wonder if Jenny still lives in the little town? I may have some of her old letters and I could get her address from them. Do you want me to look?"

"That would be great, mom. While you're doing that, I'm going to take a short nap and when I wake up, I'll have to get back to school. If you find her address, send it to me and I'll get in touch with her."

Edward went back to school, received his doctorate and was offered several jobs in various universities. He turned them all down, wanting to take some time off before he made any decisions. His mother had found Jenny's address and had called her to tell her Edward's story. Jenny had been elated to hear from her old friend after so many years and had invited them to come and visit with her. She might be able to give Edward some information about his father but she had no idea who the old woman might be. A visit was planned and soon Edward and his mother left to spend a few days with Jenny.

"Edward, I'm not sure how to tell you the way to get there. We can go along and I could show you. There are a lot of twists and turns to get to the Creek."

"Thanks, Jenny. I appreciate your willingness to show me the way but I think this is something I want to do on my own. I won't be long and if I do get lost, I can stop and ask directions. You two pretty women have a great day and I'll see you soon."

"Whatever you want. I'll draw you a rough map and maybe that will help. I've no idea of the distances so you'll have to watch the roads."

Edward followed the directions and they were pretty accurate until it was time for him to turn off to go up on the Creek. He missed the turn but stopped at a nearby house and the man there told him where to turn.

Driving slowly along the winding road and following the almost dry creek bed, he watched very carefully to find the house, which he suspected to be just ahead. How he could possibly have dreams about the house and the old woman was beyond him but he had to check it out. Something seemed to drive him along the way and he was now becoming curious about his father as well.

When he felt he was almost at the end of the paved road, he rounded a corner—and there it was!

The house was sitting very close to the road. It had a long porch across the front of it just as he saw in his dreams. There was a swing at one end and a rocker was nearby. Edward pulled up close to the house, got out of the car and knocked on the front door. It appeared no one was home but he went out back to check to see if maybe someone might be out there. Having no luck, he walked back to the front.

"Looking for somebody, sonny?"

She sat there in the rocker with her bonnet on her head and her apron tied around her waist just as he remembered in the dreams. She had a corncob pipe in her mouth and as she spoke, he could see she had no teeth.

Startled! Totally startled! Edward recovered and said, "Where in the world did you come from, ma'am? You weren't here just a minute ago."

"Oh, that's so wrong, my boy. I've been here a long time. Here, come and sit in the swing with me. I have some things to talk with you about."

"But you don't know me, or if you do, how do you know me?"

He was very uneasy about now but he walked up on the porch and took a seat in the swing.

"I don't understand this at all. I know I'm not having a dream but this is what I've been dreaming of. What's happening?"

"We don't have much time, son. You're not dreaming. This is where your father used to live and I want to talk to you about some things. The folks who live here now will be home shortly and we need to finish our conversation before they get back. You just sit there and listen to me."

Not knowing what to think, or what to do, Edward, in his confusion, sat there almost mummified. Unable to speak, he nodded to the old woman to go on. He thought perhaps she lived in the house and had seen him drive up and had come out on the porch to greet him. To himself, he said, "But how did I dream about her?"

"Listen to me, sonny. You're not here just to find out about your father, although you need to do that. There's another reason and you'll have to discover it for yourself. If you can figure it out, it will be a wonderful experience for you. If not, I can do nothing more for you."

Stammering a little, he blurted out, "But what have you done for me so far? I don't even know you and I certainly haven't seen you before unless it was while I was little. My mom says she has no idea who you might be."

"You're here, my boy, because I sent for you. Someone is also here who needs to know you. It will work out if you let it. Just don't push things and you'll be a happy young man. I can't tell you who or what is going to happen because this is something you have to work out on your own. Just know the opportunity will be there and you either will or won't take care of it. I like you and have great hopes for you."

"This is utterly nonsense. I don't know you. You don't know me. How can you say the things you've said and expect me to believe you?"

Interrupting him, the old lady spoke up. "You'll find out. You certainly will."

Looking down the road, she said, "Oh my! Here they come. They'll wonder why you're here so let's see how you handle this." She chuckled, leaned back in the swing, puffed on her pipe and told him he best go meet them.

Edward walked over to the porch steps to explain to the man and woman who were getting out of the car, who he was and why he was here. It was evident they lived here and as he got to the bottom of the steps, a very beautiful young lady got out of the back seat.

Speaking to the man, he said, "Sir. My name is Edward and I understand that once upon a time my father lived here. I came back to see if I could find any of his family since he died before I was born. No one was home except the lady there on the porch and she asked me to wait until you got here so I---"

"Mister, I don't know what you're talking about. What lady on the porch? There is no one there as far as I can see. Do you see anyone, Emma?" Speaking to his wife, he looked at Edward like he was deeply concerned to find a strange man on his porch.

"That lady right there------" Turning, he saw no one.

"What's going on here? I was just talking to an old lady sitting there in the rocker. She said you would be home shortly and I should wait. She told me she had some things to talk with me about and before she could finish, you arrived home."

Confusion was written on Edward's face as he looked at the porch, then back at the three people standing there.

The young lady spoke up. "Are you all right, Mister? Maybe I should get you a drink of water and you should sit here on the porch and rest awhile."

"No. No. I'm fine. Things are happening which I don't understand. May I sit here and tell you what I know. This is too confusing for me."

Thinking Edward had been drinking, the man carefully assisted him onto the porch and helped him sit in the swing.

"Now, Edward. Try to tell us what you're talking about. I find you sitting on my porch, you tell us you've been talking to a lady who we can't find, and you then tell us you're confused. I think you are! Or else you've been drinking too much. That sir, we don't allow here."

"No. That's not it. If you don't mind, let me tell you the events leading up to this day."

Edward told the three people about his many dreams, about the old woman who had waved to him and told him to come home to his father's family. How his mother had found an old friend who had guided him to this house. He told them who he was and how he had suddenly decided to find his father's family. When he told them who his father was, their attitude changed and they told him they were all related.

Emma asked Edward to describe the old lady to her again. Edward did so and Emma exclaimed to Ray, her husband. "That's how your grandmother looked but she's been dead for over twenty years. I don't know what's going on either but that sure enough describes granny."

Turning to Edward, she said, "And you say she was here? On the porch? Sitting here in the swing?"

"Sitting right where I am, ma'am. She was here as she was in my dreams. She also said I was not here just to find out about my father, but if I thought carefully; I would have a wonderful experience. I'm really confused and I can understand why you might think I'm drunk. I don't drink. I'm a minister, recently graduated. This is too much for me."

The young lady, Jean, looked at her father, then turning to Edward, said, "Edward, something unnatural has brought you here. Maybe we aren't supposed to understand what it is but we should think of what the message is which you're supposed to get. How you get it is unknown to any of us but surely we can discover it if we look carefully. Why don't you stay there in the swing and go over it all again with us? Maybe one of us can make some sense of your story."

"You don't believe me, do you?"

Edward was clearly uneasy. He felt rather foolish in front of these people, yet, it had happened to him and he couldn't just dismiss it.

"You'll have to admit, that it is a little hard to believe, or rather yet, to understand. Let's talk about it." And Jean sat down beside him on the swing.

The day wore on. He went over the entire story of his life as he knew it, he covered the dreams he had, and he described once again the old lady in his dreams.

"You know, folks, this is too hard to understand. I've imposed myself on you and hopefully not ruined your day. Best I get back to where mother is staying and we can leave for home in the morning. Maybe this will all go away and we can get on with our lives. Someday it may be explained to us. I think I had best go now so I thank you all for your kindness in my 'situation' and I sincerely hope I will be forgiven."

Standing up from the swing, he made a move to leave.

"Wait!" Jean smiled at him and looked at her father. "Dad, didn't you say we had no minister for church tomorrow? Let's ask Edward to give the sermon and that will give us a chance to visit some more."

"Maybe that's a good idea." Looking at Emma and seeing her nod, "Will you do it, son? We have no pressing chores and we would certainly like to hear you speak to us tomorrow. We have about fifty people in church so we aren't very big but it would be good for us to hear someone else."

"That's kind of you to ask me but mother is expecting me back in Grayson tonight and we were planning to go home in the morning. Dad is there alone and he isn't the best cook there is! He's one of the best ministers in the country but he can't wash dishes—nor can he keep house either!"

They laughed at that and then convinced him to stay, and Jean said she would go with Edward to tell his mother that he was going to preach for them tomorrow.

"Edward, I don't think mom and dad would mind for you and your mother to stay here overnight and you could leave right after church."

He agreed to ask his mom if she would stay over also, and he and Jean left for Grayson to talk with her. As they pulled out onto the road, Ray looked at Emma, "She looked a little starry eyed at him, didn't she?"

"I think so, and he was about the same with her. He seems like a nice young man, but maybe mixed up. Maybe she shouldn't have gone with him. However, how did he know about this house and Granny if he didn't have those dreams? He was never here before!"

Edward and Jean tried to convince his mother to come back with them and stay until church was over tomorrow. She wouldn't.

"Dear, I was not accepted by your father's family many years ago, and now my life has no connection to them. I'm sure Ray and Emma are lovely people because they have such a lovely daughter but I don't think I would be comfortable. Let me call your dad and see if he is all right and I'll tell him we'll be home late tomorrow night."

Jean had told them she was leaving Monday morning to try to find a job. She had graduated as an honor student in Home Health Care and was thinking about starting up her own company to care for the elderly in their own homes. She had done a lot of planning and thinking and felt she could run a successful business if she could find financial backing. There was a bank officer in Cincinnati who had agreed to talk with her about this and she was going to see him early Tuesday.

On the way back to the Creek, Edward exclaimed, "I have it! You can ride to Dayton with us and maybe dad, Dr. Penman, can give you some advice on how to proceed. He would be delighted to hear what you're trying to do. Then, if you want, I can drive you to Cincinnati Tuesday morning. How about that?"

"I don't know. We just met and wouldn't it seem funny for me to impose myself on you and your family and ask such a big favor?"

"Not at all. I have a wonderful family and my dad is a great person. He always wants to help someone and you would be the perfect person. Besides, now that I've met you, I'm not sure I want to let you go so quickly."

That brought a blush from Jean. Edward visited a long time with her family that evening. He had called his mother and asked her to speak with Ray and Emma. As he explained what he had proposed, she hesitatingly agreed to his plan.

" Edward, they don't know us and they certainly don't want their daughter going off with someone they don't know."

But Ray and Emma did agree; they knew Jean was going off by herself anyway, and she was a college graduate capable of making her own plans, and Edward and his mother seemed very genuine.

"Son, we do like you even if you have some strange dreams."

"Now I'm going to call dad and see what he thinks."

After a long discussion with his dad, Edward let Emma and Ray talk with him and then Jean. It was agreed that Jean could come and stay with them and see what she wanted to do after she talked with his dad.

"We'll be home tomorrow night, Dad."

That evening, as darkness settled in over the valley, the four of them sat on the porch listening to the night sounds of the country. Ray said he was going to bed and Jean said she had to pack. Emma sat there with Edward for awhile and talked about life on the Creek and how her life in the hills had provided many memories, but now, youth was no more, and age had entered her life, creeping up slowly and the life they once knew would be no more. Edward went off to bed to think about what he would say tomorrow in church.

Early next morning, he walked down to the meandering creek, stood and watched the morning star, the sun, rise ever higher over the hills. The time was here, and before this day was done, he felt some drastic change would come over him. The day would be entered into the pages of time as a precious memory. Had God spoken to him in his dreams? He was beginning to think so. Offering a short prayer of thanksgiving for this day, he slowly walked back to the house where the family was waiting to go with him to the church house.

Ray introduced him to the small group of parishioners and stated they were honored to have the son of Essie McGlone to be their speaker this morning. Some people didn't remember

Essie but those who did gave out a gasp, speaking out to him a big welcome. A few of these people were among those who hadn't accepted Edward's mother when his father was killed, but now they made him welcome and even asked how his mother was.

"Folks, I appreciate your welcome. I'll only speak for a few minutes. I feel that a short sermon is the best way to gain friends."

With that came laughter and loud amens.

"I had a dream last night!"

When he said this, Ray looked at Emma and Jean looked at them both, wondering what next!

"I had a dream, probably just before I woke up, that there would be an ear of corn on the banister of Ray and Emma's house. I was to take that ear of corn and preach a sermon about it. Now that is a dream to stop all dreams—well, almost anyway. When I awoke, I walked out of the house as quietly as possible, I looked at the banister and sure enough, there was an ear of corn there. I knew it wasn't there the night before so I figured Ray had been up early, had fed some of the chickens and had left the corn there. But as I walked down to the little stream, I thought, no, this is something I have to think about and how I'm supposed to preach about it. It was almost like a word from God was given to me and I had to interpret it, and do so quickly.

I still didn't know what to say as I came to church this morning and I never said a thing to Ray or Emma, nor to Jean, who I think, believes I'm a bit different anyway."

This bought a blush and a laugh from Jean.

"You see folks, I've had other dreams lately and they are what brought me to your beautiful creek to start with. I won't go into that now but here's the message I believe I'm supposed to give you this morning. This seemed to come to me as I walked in the door of your church.

Jesus told us when He was here on Earth that we should go out into the world and spread the word of the gospel. We should plant the seed, or the word, before all mankind." Breaking off a kernel, he held it up for all to see.

"Folks, as you all know, this one little kernel of corn, when treated with love and care, will create many more kernels of corn. This ear, which came from one little kernel, now provides us with many kernels. This is the way with the word of God. When you plant one tiny seed of the word and treat it with love and care, it will multiply and produce many more words, many more people to spread the word. This is what God wants of us. Be loving. Be caring. Plant the seed of His word among the people and the word will multiply and many will be saved because of that one tiny word, you, and others like you, have planted.

May God reach out his hand to guide you to a new day. Let His morning star, the sun, rise forever over your hills, and let it guide you along the paths of love. The time has come folks. Don't wait. Now, may God be with you all. Amen."

After the service, an old lady approached Edward and asked if she could speak with him for a few minutes. While the others waited for him, the lady, Mrs. Carver, spoke quietly with Edward at the back of the church.

"Edward. If I may call you Edward. That was a fine lesson you just gave us. I need to tell you that it was my family who would not accept Essie's wife, you mother, into our family. We are not related to Ray and Emma unless you go back many generations, so I don't want you to hold any hard feelings for them. I want to ask your forgiveness and I want you to tell your mother that I have prayed for forgiveness for many years. Just forgive me, son, as I pray that God will."

"Mrs. Carver. You're a grand lady to tell me this and I know that God has already forgiven you, my mother has, and rest assured that I do also. I don't want you to think about this anymore."

Edward gave her a hug and she walked off with a smile on her face.

That night Edward was having dreams again. The old lady, Granny, again appeared to him.

"Remember sonny, when I told you that the reason you had been called to the Creek was for an experience I couldn't explain at the time? Well, you've had, and are having, that experience. What will you do with it?" She then disappeared, fading away into his dream.

Next day, Edward and his mother went back to their home. They took Jean with them and she spent several hours talking with Edward's father about what she wanted to do. Being a much-respected minister in the area, he had some contacts he referred her to, and told Edward he had found Jean to be a charming and a very ambitious young lady.

Jean went on to become a successful business lady in the home health care business and Edward took a position at a local university and preached every Sunday at one of the small churches in the area. He felt his calling was to minister to the smaller churches that never had the finances to hire a full time minister. He never accepted a fee.

Granny faded out of his dreams, never to appear again.

*****

Edward and Jean were married two years later!

OUR CHRISTMAS TREE

I don't remember how old I was. Perhaps ten and my only brother, Ryan, must have been twelve. We had two older sisters, Betty and Patti, but at our ages, sisters didn't count.

One day in early November, mom told us to go out and play and to get out from under her feet!

"Why don't you boys go back in the woods and pick out a Christmas tree? It won't be long until time to bring one in. If you can find it now in warm weather, it will be a lot easier on you when the snow comes."

We were only too anxious to go. We had always gone to pick out our tree since we were barely old enough to walk. Dad would hitch up one of the horses to a wagon and load us in the back with our sisters and off we would go. We'd follow the wagon trail as it wound back into the woods and pick out the tree we wanted. Dad would mark it by tying a cloth around the top and when Christmas time came, we would go back and get it. Of course we always had arguments with the sisters about which tree we should take and Ryan and I always lost.

The girls were twins and were four years older than Ryan so this particular year, they were about sixteen. They had stopped going with us a year or so before, preferring to stay home and decorate the tree   when we brought it in. Dad would go, saying we were still too young to go alone with the horses and wagon.

Of course Ryan disagreed, knowing he was now a 'man.' Ryan and me got along pretty well. I thought he was something special and he had me convinced he knew everything. I think it had really hurt his pride for dad to go with us this year.

Now, Christmas was only a few days away, but in November, when mom told us to go pick out a tree, we hurried off and stopped at Cousin Jerry's house to see if he wanted to go with us. Aunt Mildred, Jerry's mom told us not to be late since Jerry had some chores to do before dark.

Away we went with the spirit of the wind, knowing we would get the very best tree there was in the woods, and mom and dad would be so proud of us. Ryan led the way with Jerry and me following behind. He kept telling us to be careful of any animals, which might creep up on us. We knew there were no dangerous animals around but since Ryan told us to be careful, we naturally let our imagination take over and watched and listened carefully.

The day wore on and we pretended we were deep in some strange forest being very careful of, what Ryan said, were bears creeping up behind us. Ryan picked up a large stick and told Jerry and me to do the same and told me to walk behind and to watch carefully so we wouldn't be surprised. He sent Jerry ahead to be our 'scout.'

We arrived at our 'forest' of cedar trees and ran through all of them looking for the perfect tree. Suddenly, a yell from Jerry!

"I've found it! I've found it! Come look at this one."

We hurried over to where he was and both agreed it was a beautiful tree. Ryan walked around the tree, looking carefully at its branches.

"O.K. Let's mark it so we can find it when we come back. Give me the cloth, Mark."

"I don't have the cloth. Didn't you get it off the side of the well?"

Ryan looked at me, "No. I thought you had it."

I felt so badly, I remember I was about ready to cry.

As usual, Ryan to the rescue!

"Here. We'll put this big stick up beside it and that way we can find it when we come back. Let's set it right here."

And he leaned the stick up against the tree. Of course we never thought of any wind coming along which might blow the stick over. And that's probably what happened because we never found the tree when we came to cut it down. We had a big snow four days before Christmas and dad hooked up the sleigh instead of the wagon and this year, we all went for a ride. Mom had dressed us up in our warm clothes and Ryan sat up front with dad so he could tell him how to get to the tree. After we had ridden for a long time, Ryan had to admit he didn't remember where the tree was and asked me to help out.

"I don't know, Ryan. You put the stick by the tree and said you could see it from the road."

"Now that's all right, boys." Dad put his arm around Ryan and smiled back at me. "We can find another real soon."

The girls had to get their sassy remarks in at us but mom quieted them down.

Soon we had picked out another tree and loaded it onto the sleigh and headed for home. Ryan and I did our chores while the girls and mom decorated the tree. Dad had filled a bucket with coal and we put the tree in the bucket using the coal to hold the tree up straight. We had some sycamore balls, which mom had covered with tinfoil to hang on the tree and our sisters cut out some red and green paper and glued them in circles to hang along with the balls. We also had strings of popcorn to wrap around the branches. When it was done, it was the prettiest of all trees.

That evening, five of us sat around the tree and warmed ourselves by the fireplace, while mom made lots of popcorn. When it was all popped, dad took a pot of molasses and held it over the fire and let it soften into a semi liquid. He then poured the popcorn into the large pot and using his hands, he stirred it all up and made popcorn balls. He rolled them up and placed them on the table to cool. While this was going on, mom had made some 'taffy pull' candy and the six of us had the pleasant task of pulling on the candy until it was just the right consistency. It was so very good and mom let us all have a bite before it cooled down.

Dad lit the kerosene lamps and we gathered around the fire and he read the Christmas story to us. Each Christmas since I could remember, he read this story to us, and then he would sit and play the organ as we joined in to sing, SILENT NIGHT. Sure, momma had heard the story before but each year it seemed to get better and we could imagine ourselves as shepherds and seeing the bright star. Ryan and me said we would be good shepherds and wouldn't be afraid if we were alone out in the fields. Our sisters had to chime in that we were afraid to even go to the barn after dark.

"We're not either!" I opened my mouth too quickly. "We saw you and those two boys, Will and Sammy, down in the barn a few nights ago."

Oh! I could have cut my tongue out!

Mom and dad looked at each other, then at the two girls.

"Well!" Mom yelled out at them. "Young ladies, what do you have to say for yourselves?"

Had looks been able to kill, I would have been dead that Christmas Eve. Sister Betty looked at me, then at Sister Patti, and they both began to cry.

"Momma! Nothing happened. We told Will and Sammy we would talk with them and they wanted to meet us at the barn. We did. We just talked and told them we had to get back to the house and they left right away. We did nothing wrong other than slipping out of the house without you knowing. We're sorry, Momma. That's all there was to it."

Dad, with his stern face, looked at the girls and then to me.

"Mother, if Betty and Patti say nothing happened, then nothing did."

Turning to the girls again.

"Betty, you and Patti are too young to know much about life, although me and your mother were married when we were just a little older. We older folk sometimes forget what it is like to be young and pretty. We care for you both very much and we only want to see that no harm comes to you. I think you've learned your lesson and maybe we can sit here by the fire and talk things over after Christmas. I think your mother will want to talk to you also, but that can wait. Right now, we're talking about Christmas and the Christ Child."

Mom walked over to Betty and Patti, put her arms around them and motioned for Ryan and me to come to her. We all stood there wrapped in each other's arms, crying, laughing, and finally realizing that this was what Christmas was all about. Loving one another and helping each other through difficult times.

I looked at the girls and said, "I'm sorry. I didn't mean to spy but I had to go out to the outhouse and I saw you two going to the barn and I wondered why and followed you. I won't do it again. I promise!"

Betty chimed in. "We won't do it again either."

Dad sat there in his rocker with the contented look on his face that we all had learned to recognize. It was such a joy to sit with dad and mom by the fire and listen to them talk about the days where they were younger. Dad would tell us stories about the things he and his father would do and Ryan and me would remember these and try to do them ourselves next day. Many exciting adventures came to us because of our imagining the things we were doing.

"Well, children!" Dad held us all close. "Tomorrow is Christmas Day, the Day we celebrate the birth of Jesus. Tradition says we are to exchange gifts. You know we've never had much to give to you and this year is no different. But I want you all to remember that what we do have, we give to you because we love you. Don't ever forget that mother and me love you all and if we could, we would give you the finest presents in the whole world.

Now it's bedtime and we all must get up in the morning and do our chores. The cows still have to be milked, the eggs gathered, the horses and hogs fed. We need to make sure the dogs and cats have something to eat. Mother says she will fix us a big breakfast and that will do for our presents. Maybe someday, you can all marry some rich men and women and have all the gifts you want. Don't forget now, we love all four of you."

Dad stood up, walked over to mom, gave her a big hug and said it was his bedtime. "Merry Christmas to all!"

He walked up the stairs to his bedroom and as we watched him go, we felt so loved. You could feel a sense of love in the air. We all hugged and said goodnight. The girls again assured me that it was all right I had told on them and I again told them I was sorry. Mom shooed us all to bed and then she set the fire for the night, and put out all the kerosene lamps except the one she carried upstairs to the bedroom.

Ryan and I talked awhile about what we would get under the tree tomorrow. He said it would probably be an orange and an apple with taffy candy and popcorn balls. I didn't care what it was. I was so happy to be a part of this family that night. I soon dropped off to sleep and I suppose Ryan did also, because a deep quietness settled over the house.

Christmas morning came. We hurried down the stairs to the tree and mom was already busy in the kitchen making biscuits. Dad was down at the barn milking and the girls were gathering the eggs in the hen house.

"Why didn't you wake us, Mom?" Ryan felt he had missed something by not being up early.

"Dear, I was busy cooking. I felt you two needed your rest today and thought it best you sleep in."

Dad came in with the girls and the family sat around the big dining table as mom served up generous portions of ham and eggs. MY GOODNESS! And she had put some jams on the table to eat with the biscuits she had baked. I remember we all did our share in the eating department. Dad gave a prayer and mom led us in a Christmas song. I've forgotten which one, and then we all laughed as we filled our plates. No one really cared that all each of us got under the tree was an orange along with the candy and popcorn balls. I remembered what Ryan had said the night before and he was right. His being right again just increased my childish awe of him.

Breakfast was finally over and mom and the girls started to clean up the dishes and Ryan and I started to the barn to feed the horses. Dad spoke up. "Boys, I fed the horses while I was doing the milking and Betty, you and Patti are getting the day off. I'm going to help mother with the dishes and then we'll get together with Jerry's folks this afternoon. Why don't you children go down to the creek to see if it's frozen over? We may want to do some fishing this afternoon. It's cold out so dress warmly."

We ran to get our coats and hats and dashed out of the house to run to the creek. Fishing with dad was one of our really pleasant times. Usually Betty and Patti enjoyed it also. They probably didn't want to fish if it was cold but they went along with us anyway. The creek wasn't frozen over and if we had thought about it, we would have known it wasn't before we went down there. It was not at all cold; actually I remember it was rather warm for December. There was no snow, no ice and we didn't need our heavy coats. We ran back to the house to tell mom and dad that it was warm, too warm for ice. But maybe we could go fishing anyway.

The four of us ran into the house, into the kitchen, and then into the parlor where mom and dad sat by the fire. Dad didn't smoke much but today he had his pipe lit and mom was doing some mending of clothes.

"There's no ice, dad, and we don't have any snow. Can we go fishing anyway?"

I was excited and didn't even bother to look around.

Suddenly, it became quiet in the room. No one said anything, no one breathed. Finally, gasps came from the four of us. Sitting off in a corner by the tree were four of the most wonderful red and yellow bicycles there were!

Mom and dad sat there and smiled while we all ran to the bicycles and then back to mom, to dad, and back to the bicycles. Talk about a state of confusion. No one could say anything!

"Can we ride them, Dad? Mom, can we go try them out?"

Words seemed to come faster than we could say them. It didn't occur to us that mom and dad had saved all year long to be able to buy us the bicycles. That wasn't important right now. The fact that we had our life long dream was nearly more than we could handle.

Off we raced, realizing finally that dad had sent us to the creek so he could get the bicycles out of their hiding place.

Happy?

Oh my goodness! Never were there four happier children!

That Christmas Day passed, as did the winter. With the coming of spring, planting had to be done and the farm chores increased. We all worked hard and after the chores were done, we would race our bicycles up and down the little dirt road in front of the house. A few cars would go by and dad always cautioned us to be careful. In August, mom was preparing some dishes for the reunion to be held at the church house the next Sunday. Ryan had gone to see Jerry, and Betty and Patti were on the porch with two boys. I was pumping up a tire on my bicycle when a car came speeding up the road. The driver stopped and yelled for dad to come quickly.

Jerry and Ryan had been playing on the hill down behind the creek, and both had fallen off a cliff into a deep part of the water. Evidently they had hit their heads on a boulder in the water and both were killed instantly.

*****

I grew up and left the Creek when I was nineteen. War had come along and I had been drafted. I was gone for three years and when I came back, things were not the same. The girls had married two fine young men but mom and dad were different. I didn't know why and I asked Patti what was wrong. She didn't know but thought they both were real sick. They wouldn't talk about it to her so finally I made up my mind to ask them.

"You know, mom and dad, I love you. I love you so much that sometimes it hurts me deep inside when I'm away. It hurt when we lost Ryan, and now Betty and Patti are gone, and I suppose I may leave someday. I'm not cut out to be a farmer. I don't know why but I don't want to do that kind of work."

I walked over to them, sitting side by side in the swing and put my arms around them.

"Tell me what's wrong. Maybe I can help."

Mom and dad put their arms around each other, looked into the other's eyes, and both smiled at me. Mom moved over and let me sit between them on the swing.

"No, sonny. You can't help us. It's too late. The doctor says your father has emphysema and has only a little while to live, maybe just days. We didn't want to tell any of you but I suppose it's best we do."

Dad held my hand and softly said, " I wanted to live until you got home so I could see you again, and now that you're here, I think it best for all that I go on. I don't want to suffer any more nor do I want to cause your mother any more problems than I already have. She's been an angel to take such good care of me."

Mother started to cry and said she loved taking care of him.

Dad went on. "I guess the tobacco finally got to me and I have to pay the price. I have no fears since I feel God will care of me. I don't want you to be sad at my going. Have a big smile because of your remembering what we all had."

I cried then! I had to go away and cry. I went to the barn, saddled a horse and rode across the ridge in front of the house. I sat under a large pine tree looking down the ridge toward the house. Mom and dad were still sitting there in the swing. No one could have loved me more than they did and no one could have loved them more that me. Just before dark I rode back, put the horse in the barn, walked up to the house feeling like my life had ended in this valley. I could not stay here after dad was gone and I meant to tell them this evening—but I couldn't! It seemed too final, too morbid, for me to tell them I was leaving them.

We lost dad three weeks later and mom soon followed. I left the Creek and never saw my sisters again until I was sixty-two years old. Something like forty years had passed. But I couldn't go back.

Now, time has called me home and here I am back in the valley, walking down the narrow dirt road early one morning.

Dawn was breaking!

The gray of the clouds turned to a crimson red as I walked through the meadow, past the old walnut tree where as a youngster, I had picked walnuts and carried them home to mother. She would take a hammer and remove the hard shell and keep the nuts in a jar until time came to make candy for Christmas. As I moved through the dew covered grass, my feet felt the wetness of the morning and I wondered if the cow path I once knew so well would still be there. The old barbed wire fence was still attached to the rotting posts and as I stepped over the wire. There it was! Still used by cows, the path was as worn as it had been those many years ago.

Avoiding the cow pies, I climbed slowly to the top, watching to see if there was anyone else moving on the hill. It was quiet, almost too quiet. A woodpecker made an occasional 'peck peck' noise but nothing more.

Now, standing on the crest of the hill, I looked down on the valley floor. The long, lonely narrow dirt road was winding through fresh, new growth —the leaves were almost fully out on the trees, flowers were blooming, lilac bushes planted in bygone days were beginning to show their magnificent colors and the redbud and dogwood of the hills, were magnifying the beauty of the Creek.

Shortly, these morning mists in the valley below, began their rise up the hillside, sometimes covering the great oaks of the forest, sometimes shining in the morning sun. The little creek flowed through the tree-lined banks and the water glistened like a satin ribbon threading its way through a veil of green.

Memories? Beautiful dreams of days gone by filled my soul. I stood there on the rocky cliff and listened to the loneliest song of all, the wind. There…off in the meadow, the bob white sang its wake up song as the morning star rose ever higher. Like all the others before it, when this day is done, it will be entered into the pages of time as a precious memory—never to relive, but always to remember. But none as great as that day, that Christmas Day, about fifty years ago, when I received my bicycle.

BEE DEE AND DEE DEE

The old iron potbelly stove was still standing in the center of the room. The stovepipe ran up to the ceiling and out the trap door leading to Abe's upstairs storage. Spring was here but Abe, the storekeeper, had not yet bothered to remove it for the spring and summer.

"That thing needs to be moved out of here, Abe. Takes too much room from our chairs. Where are we going to sit while it's still here?"

"Instead of thinking about chairs, best you buy something, Hank. I can certainly use the business." Abe and Hank, friends from years past, laughed. They were alone in Abe's small general merchandise store, located about twenty miles from the County Seat of Grayson.

Outside, the weather was almost too wet for anyone to be out. The rain was blowing sideways and the big drops were rolling along the saturated ground. Abe had the only store left in the little village and he doubled as the local postmaster, a job he had kept for over twenty years. Usually on a Saturday morning, his store was filled with customers, local loafers, and some who were waiting for him to complete putting the mail in boxes.

"I 'spect some folks to come in later, Hank. That old Mrs. Howard is one for getting her mail on time." Abe giggled when he said that. "And she lets you know about it if it's not here when she comes in. I don't look for her today, though."

"I don't know about that. Somebody's coming in the door now."

A blast of rain sent droplets into the door way as Abe went to the door and helped open it. Heavy thunder sounded in the hills and lightning lit up the darkened sky at ten o'clock in the morning.

"Why howdy, Stan. That you, Herb? What are you two doing out on a day like this?"

"Good morning, Abe. There's two or three more just behind us. Better wait here by the door to let them in."

Stan shook the rain off his shoulders, stomped his feet and hung his hat and coat on the coat rack near the door.

"It was either come to see you down here or stay home and clean house for the Missus. Herb stopped by and said he had to get some groceries so I thought I'd mosey along with him. Say, that stove is a bit in the way, isn't it?" Going right on without waiting for an answer, he said, "This is quite a day we have here. Probably won't have any mail today. Raining too hard for the postman to drive the roads."

"I doubt if we will." Herb looked over at Abe to see if he had heard anything about the delivery today.

"Haven't heard a word except they told me in Grayson that Elmer left on time but he may not make it out here. I 'spect it's flooding quite a bit down by Ellie Carroll's place. They need to fix that road. Make it higher."

Abe opened the door and let in three more men.

"Howdy, boys. Now don't tell me that stove is in the way! I'm trying to get time to move it but right now I have too many customers."

"Just a minute ago, you said you needed the business, Abe. Reckon you can't make up your mind." Hank looked at Stan and winked.

Clay, Bruce, and Carlos entered, shook off the water, removed their coats and boots and pulled up chairs near the stove.

"That stove's in........"

"Don't say it, Clay. Abe's already complaining about the stove. Says he's too busy to move it. Has too many customers."

"Well now, Abe, I don't see many customers in here right now. Why don't you move it out and we will all watch and see that you do a good job?"

Carlos had joined in the fun, and Abe, good-natured as he was, joined them in laughing.

The phone rang, and after answering it, Abe told them that Elmer could not get through on his route today so there would be no mail.

"The water is too deep down at Ellie's and he said he would see us on Monday."

"Just as well. I guess we won't have to pay the bills if we don't get them." Stan seemed to be in a good mood and all the men laughed at him when he spoke of paying the bills.

Times were not good out on the Creek, but the men gathered in Abe's store were all retired and most of them had a somewhat comfortable living. That was not always the case however. For the most part, they were farmers and some had done well with tobacco through the years.

Stan had been the school principal and Clay had been the County Clerk. The others were still part time farmers with side jobs like blacksmithing, painting, and driving the school busses in the area.

"Stan, we're all sitting here doing nothing so why don't you tell us a story. You always have something to say about the Creek. That'll help pass the time before we have to go home for dinner." Carlos was always ready to volunteer others for some job. He was well liked by the men and mostly they listened to him.

The others chimed in. "Go ahead, Stan. Either tell us a story or we'll call the missus and tell her you're down here loafing so you won't have to help her."

"I almost believe I'd rather do housework today than be associated with a bunch of men like you!" They all laughed as they pulled their chairs around in a circle. Some lit pipes and others just leaned back to get comfortable.

"All right. You asked for it! I believe I'll tell you a story of Bee Dee and Dee Dee." Pausing, Stan seemed deep in thought and then he started his story.

"This happened a long time ago when I was a young father and just beginning to teach school here on the Creek. My goodness, that was a long time ago! I don't remember if any of you were around then or not. Abe, I believe you were. Weren't you in one of my classes?"

"Stan, I was in your first school. I was in the second grade and sure was scared when you got your little willow switch out and laid it on the desk. Looked to me like you meant business. You would pull your glasses down onto your nose and we didn't know if you were reading or watching us."

Looking up, "Well, here's Stu. Come on in, Stu. Pull up a chair. Stan is telling us another one of his stories."

"Howdy, fellows. Goodness, Abe, that stove is sure in the way!"

Everybody laughed as Abe opened the door of the store and invited them to help move the stove.

"No volunteers? Well, that does it! Stan, hurry with your story so I can sweep all these here fellers out in the rain."

Abe stood in the door of his store, looking at the nearby hills. "See that lightning? Maybe it will strike up on the hill. I certainly hope not."

Stan went on.

"I think you all know I have two sons. When they were little, I promised them both a puppy when they were six years old. Corey was the oldest and Glen the younger by two years. On Corey's sixth birthday, I brought home two puppies from Mack Johnson's dog, Sadie. That Sadie was a good 'coon hunter with a great nose. I had decided I would get Glen's at the same time and let them

46

grow up together. I had also promised the boys to take them 'coon hunting when they got to the age of six. Corey was six in May and mother and I decided that a good time to take them hunting would be the night of the full moon in October. That way it would be bright out and they probably wouldn't be as scared to be in the woods. October came along and the puppies were growing but still too small to do much hunting. However, I wanted them to get used to being in the woods so on the night of the harvest moon, I packed up some sandwiches, got our old tent, and off we went. We would do no hunting this year but it would be fun to be there in the open with Corey. I tried to get Glen to understand he couldn't go until he was six."

Stan interrupted his story.

"Howdy, Miss Howard. Best you come on in and shake the water off and listen to my story. Won't be any mail today but my story will be better than the mail anyway."

He chuckled to himself as Miss Howard said she didn't understand why the mail couldn't come through, harrumphed, and left the store.

"She's quite a woman, isn't she, Abe?" Clay walked to the door to see if it was still raining as hard as it was earlier.

"She certainly is. But she is really good hearted. If you need something, she is right there to help out. Go on with your story, Stan."

"It was a great night. We built a little fire; cooked some hot dogs and I fixed his bed for him. I sat there on the hillside for quite a while before turning in. Over between the hill behind Herb's and Carl's, I saw one of the most beautiful sights I have ever seen. The big full moon began to rise over the valley and for just a minute it seemed to sit right on the horizon blazing with its red color. Then it slowly crept into the sky and the entire valley lit up almost like day. Right then and there, I promised myself that the boys and me would always go hunting on the night of the harvest moon. I wanted them to be outside to share the gift God gave us. And, with the exception of the nights when it rained or was too cloudy to see the moon, we always went to that hillside. When Glen was six, he joined us and by then the puppies were full grown dogs of two years and they were off romping in the hills enjoying the fun of being up there with us.

"Did you ever actually go 'coon hunting, Stan?" Carlos interrupted as he got a drink from the cooler.

"We never went hunting. I never believed in killing animals unless they were to eat and I guess I never cared for 'coon meat. We kept this up for years. The boys grew into young men and the dogs were like brothers to them. They never went anywhere without the dogs. We were seldom disappointed by the weather. I think once we had a little snow so we didn't go and maybe four or five of the years it either rained or was cloudy, so like I said, we didn't go then either. As they grew older, we would walk around the hillside, sometimes trying to follow the dogs, but usually we just walked and talked.

The years went quickly by and suddenly they were in high school and their interests were changing. I could tell it but they never planned anything on 'our' night, even missing a ball game once, much to the displeasure of the coach. Then came graduation for Corey and off to college. I figured the trips to the hill would be over, at least for him, but he surprised me and came home for our annual trip. The next year Glen had joined Corey in school and for the first time since they were six, they failed to join me on the hill. I went! I took the two dogs and off we went to see the moon come up. The dogs were now fourteen years old and their roaming days were about over.

I guess I neglected to tell you their names. When Corey saw his puppy for the first time, he said his name would be Bee Dee. I don't know why the Bee Dee but that's what he called him. Glen heard him say that and he picked up his puppy and said his name would be Dee Dee. Those two names stuck and no one ever figured out why.

Anyway, the next year came and both of the boys said they were coming home for their night on the hill. What mother and I didn't know was, they were bringing two girls with them. Lovely young ladies they were, but when it came time to go up the hill, both boys said the girls couldn't go, it was their night and maybe the girls could go some other time.

Mother fixed us some tasty sandwiches and gave me instructions not to get cold, told the boys to watch out that I didn't fall and some other things I've forgotten, and off we went. The dogs, overjoyed to see the boys, ran along with us but when we got to the bottom of the hill, Bee Dee fell and had trouble getting up. Corey went to him, picked him up, talked to him a little, and carried him in his arms the rest of the way."

"Dad, has Bee Dee been having trouble?"

"Corey, best you know. Bee Dee has been falling quite a bit lately. He will rest for a while and then get up and try to go on, but it's getting awfully hard for him. This may be his last trip up the hill. I'm sorry but he is getting quite old."

Corey said to Bee Dee, as he walked on ahead. "C'mon old fellow, let's me and you go look at the moon. You won't have to do a thing but sit with me by the fire and watch the night sky."

"They went on up the hill to our camping spot and Corey spread his blanket, sat down, took Bee Dee in his arms and it appeared they were looking off over the valley to watch for the rising of the moon. Bee Dee lay there on Corey's lap while Dee Dee and Glen went to get some fire wood."

Corey called out to Glen. "Glen, let's not have a fire right now. I think we can see the moon better if it's dark when it comes up."

"That's fine with me. Is it all right with you, Dad?"

"Whatever you boys want is fine with me. This is your night and I suspect it may be the last time the three of us and the dogs ever do this. Those two girls down at the house have stars in their eyes and I believe those stars are you boys. How about that?"

Corey laughed. "Dad, I was going to tell you and mom tomorrow that Katie and I are engaged so when I do, don't tell her you know. I'll finish school and so will she."

"Hey! There it comes. Look at that moon! Has it ever been bigger that this?"

Glen jumped up and moved over to a large boulder, climbed it and called for us to join him.

"You go ahead, Dad. I'll stay here with Bee Dee. I think he needs me right now. Look at Dee Dee. She seems to know Bee Dee isn't well."

"Dogs seem to have a way of sensing something isn't right. You stay here. I'll go over with Glen."

Shortly, the moon had risen high into the sky, the whippoorwills were singing in the valley and down by the creek, the frogs were singing along with the insects of the night. The bats were busy flying around us and down in the barn, we could hear a barn owl calling out. We stretched our sleeping bags out on the ground and the three of us secretly knew that this was going to be our last night for watching the moon. Oh, maybe someday, we would all be together and come back up here but this was our last time on a schedule. The boys were now young men, off in college, busy with their studying, and of course, girls were now a big part of their life. Soon, they would be off on their own, working in perhaps distant places and the Creek would only be a fond memory.

They finally had built a small fire while sitting there talking. When bedtime came, Corey said he would put out the fire after Glen and I went to bed. The night had grown late and it was time to get some sleep. Corey stood up, poured some water on the little fire, and in the brightness of the night, started to get into his sleeping bag. Bee Dee had been curled up in his arms and moved slowly when Corey got up. When he returned to his bed, Bee Dee didn't move.

She died there that night at the age of fifteen. Corey spoke to us quietly saying, "Dad and Glen, I've just lost my best friend."

Nothing was said by anyone for a while. Dee Dee came over to where Corey and Bee Dee were, sniffed a bit and then began an almost human cry. She knew that Bee Dee was no more. Corey got up and walked over to the tree line and we could hear his sobbing. Both Glen and I stayed where we were. Glen held Dee Dee tightly and finally I went over to Corey, took him one of our camp shovels and suggested he bury Bee Dee there on the hill under the harvest moon. I put my arm around him and he hugged me, took the shovel, walked off by himself carrying Bee Dee. After some time passed, we saw him returning to our camp.

"Dad, I can't stay up here tonight. Let's go back home, or if you want to stay with Glen, I'll go by myself."

Glen hurriedly agreed that it would be best if we all went back, so we walked down the hill silently, guided by the light of the moon. I had tears in my eyes because I too, had loved the dogs, but mostly I felt sorrow because of the hurt felt by Corey. Mother and the girls met us at the door and we all had some silent moments before we turned in for the night.

Early next morning, I found Corey down by the creek bank with Glen and Dee Dee. Corey said it would be best for him if he left for school right away.

"I can't stay here right now, Dad. I'll be back for Thanksgiving and will bring Katie if you don't care. I'll tell mom about our being engaged and then I believe we'll leave. I hope you understand."

"You ago ahead, son. Whatever you feel is best for you. Glen, if you feel you must leave, feel free to go also. I'll take good care of Dee Dee for you."

They both left that morning. It was quiet, too quiet in the house. Mother and I took a walk out to the barn. We called and called for Dee Dee but she was nowhere to be found. I said I thought I knew where she was, so we walked up the hill and found the spot where Corey had buried Bee Dee. There lay Dee Dee on the fresh ground Corey had dug. I called to her, she started to come to me, but she turned and went back and lay down again on the ground.

"Girl, you can't stay here. C'mon now, let's go home."

She looked at me, whined, and then she closed her eyes and she died. Right there, on the same spot where Bee Dee had been buried. Mother went back to the house to get a shovel while I stayed with the dogs. Finally I couldn't take it anymore and tears rolled down my cheeks, as I knew a part of my life had come to an end. My boys had grown up and left home, as they should have; the two dogs I had raised from puppies had died, and now only Mother and I remained in the big house.

I don't go back up the hill anymore. Nor do the boys. They come home but make it a point not to come on the night of the harvest moon. We still listen to the night creatures and sometimes I can stand outside and hear 'coon dogs running the hills. I wonder if old Bee Dee and Dee Dee aren't calling out to the boys and me. They sure were good dogs.

I guess that's the end of my story for now fellows. Hope I didn't bore you. Look out there! The rain has stopped!

Time to be getting home."

JIM

Thundering hoof beats sounded down the valley, muffled by the hills lining each side of the creek. The two riders, Tex and Silver, with guns blazing, rode their mounts across the open field and up a little hill, in hot pursuit of two bandits who had just held up the local bank.

Suddenly, just ahead of them------------!

"Who ye boys be, anyways? Whut ye be doin' up on my hill?"

Scared, the two boys dropped their stick mounts and started to run away. A big hand reached out and grabbed one of them gently by his collar. "Did ye not hear me? Who air ye boys?"

"I'm Douglas Stanton's boy. This is…."

"Ye be Uncle Doug's boy? Waal now, I don't rightly rekken he'd be awantin' ye to be up hyar. I tell ye whut we'll do. Now you two fellers jest go on back down the hill and don' be acomin' up hyar no more 'an I won't be atellin' yore pa."

The man seemed nine feet tall and his black beard looked like it hung to the ground. He had a big long rifle cradled in an arm, and to the boys, he seemed like the devil himself.

"Go on now. Scat outta hyar."

The two boys, who recently were Tex and Silver, were now Ralph and Ken. Instead of chasing bank robbers, they were now two very scared lads. They ran down the hill and out across the field toward the barn where they usually played. Both were nine years old and Ken was visiting Ralph while their fathers did some work on the farmhouse.

Douglas and his brothers and sisters were born in the house and now the older brother, Marv, lived there. The brothers would visit as often as possible, always wanting to come back to the home place. Doug, Marv and Harry were brothers, three of eleven children born to Conn and Suzy, there in the valley.

Ralph stopped running, started to cry, and Ken ran back to him to see what was wrong.

"I wuz plum scared, Ken. I peed in my pants and ma is shore to ask me what made me do it. I can't go back into the house until my pants dry out."

"Let's go down to the creek and go swimming. You can hang your pants in a tree and they can dry while we swim. You can even tell your mom we splashed water on them, if you want."

"I can't tell her a lie, Ken. I can't."

The boys slowed down to a walk as they neared the creek bank.

"Who was that man, Ralph? He sure was scary looking. I'm not going to tell my dad and don't you say anything either. Dad wouldn't be too happy if he knew what we did."

"I'd get me a whopping fer shore if pa found out. I'll keep quiet, Ken. Let's go swimming."

*****

A car pulled over to the side of the road where a grocery store once sat, just off the bridge which crossed the little stream of water. A tall gray haired man opened the door, got out and moved over to the creek bank as he eyed the valley up ahead. Memories flooded the mind of the man. He recalled those haunting winds of so many years ago, which in his mind, caused ghosts and spirits of the past to swarm between the hills. The squeaking trees as the wind raced through the branches, the hooting of the owls from down in the barn, the dark tombstones of the cemetery as he passed by in the night; ghosts and spirits, his brothers had told him. Sometimes scared to tears, he would run home where his ma would hold and cuddle him, and scold his brothers for what they had done.

Ken was back in the valley to attend the annual reunion, his first trip back in almost forty years.   He would meet his dad up at the old home place and they would spend the night with Marv. Doug had faithfully come to the reunions over the years, but now he was getting very old and this would probably be his last trip. He had asked Ken, his oldest son, if he could make the trip back to the valley this year, and Ken had been only too happy to join his dad there.

On Saturday evening, the day before the reunion, Doug, Marv and Harry, were sitting on the front porch of the old home and were reminiscing about the early days in the valley. Ken listened to them awhile and then spoke up, telling his adventures as a youngster up on the hill back of the house.

Marv spoke, "Doug, that must have been Sister Ida's boy, Jim. I don't know anyone else who might have lived up there."

"That's probably who it was. I remember Jim. I had him in school for a year or two and then he quit. His sister Phoebe, was a year or two older and she came to school a bit longer that he did. Neither one of them learned much."

Doug sat in the swing with Harry; Marv was sitting on the steps of the porch. A light rain began to fall and Marv moved back to a chair as the raindrops pounded on the tin roof. Back up the valley, a whippoorwill was singing and down in the barn, there was the occasional hoot of an owl. Ken reminded them of how they used to scare him with their ghost tales!

"Harry, remember when Ida was going out with Hubert? She got herself in trouble and when Hubert found out, he was going to leave the valley. I believe it was you who went up on the hill to make sure he never left, wasn't it?"

Harry stood up from the swing, walked over to the porch railing, and pounded his pipe against a post. He looked over the farm and turned to Doug and Marv.

"Hubert never amounted to much. He came from a bad family and he kept the mean streak in him. I never did figure out what Ida saw in him but she always told me she didn't want anyone else. I had a little talk with Hubert. It was really more than a talk, and he never came to see me after that. My goodness! That was long time ago. Ida sure had a rough time but she wouldn't let us interfere. I think you were the only one who could go up to see her, Doug. I don't know why that was, but even Hubert respected you."

"I don't know why he did either. He certainly respected no one else. The last year I taught school here, both Jim and Phoebe came to me and told me they wouldn't be back school. Said their pa needed them on the farm. I went up to see Ida and Hubert, and Ida looked like she was in bad shape. She was stooped over, her hair was a mess, and when I asked her what was wrong, she said she was just fine. Hubert said he would walk me to the road and I saw the look he gave Ida. I should have insisted that she come with me but then I never liked to interfere unless I was asked. I always wanted to do to Hubert what Harry had done, and that was the day I should have done it. She died a few days later."

Marv spoke up. "Hubert never did a bit of farming in his life except to grow some corn to make that 'shine. I imagine he made Ida do most of the farm work. I heard later that he was downright mean to her. We should have done something back then but I guess we were all the same. We didn't want to interfere. And she could have walked away most anytime she wanted to. We would have welcomed her home.

When Hubert died, Jim came down to the house to tell me about it and said he had buried his pa next to Ida. I wanted to go up to see the graves but Jim acted like he didn't want me to so I just put it off. I never did see Phoebe but Jim said she was doing all right."

Marv walked over to the edge of the porch and looked at the sky.

"There are some stars coming out so the rain must be about over. I expect we'll have a good crowd here tomorrow. I'm going to bed, Doug. I'll see you all tomorrow."

Harry also got up and walked out on the front lawn, got in his buggy and drove off. Harry, the oldest of the three living brothers, never accepted the automobile. Said he would have no reason to leave the valley and the buggy would take him wherever he wanted to go.

Doug and Ken sat there and began talking about some of the happenings in the valley.

"Dad, tell me about this cousin of mine, Jim. What happened to him, and also, what happened to Phoebe?"

"You've been gone a long time from here, Ken. I've been away a while also. Memories grow dim but I'll tell you the story as I remember it.

Our sister, Ida, was bull headed. She wanted to marry Hubert and she didn't care what she did to get him. I think she purposely got herself pregnant just to make him marry her. She knew Marv and Harry would make Hubert marry her when they found out. Hubert was a moon shiner and not a good one at that. He was mean, in fact, his whole family was mean. There was no law out here in the valley and there was always trouble with Hubert's family. Finally, some of the farmers around here went calling on them and almost beat Hubert's pa to death. Some say his pa died as a result of the beating.

Hubert and Ida had two children, Phoebe and Jim. Many said Phoebe wasn't 'right in the head' and I suspect that was true. She wasn't a very pretty girl. She had red hair like her mother but the rest of her was just like Hubert. She learned a few things in school very quickly, but other things came very slowly, if at all. She would try hard to read but never could.

Jim was tall and skinny. He never shaved and seldom bathed as far as I could tell. He learned the moonshine trade from Hubert.

About once a month in the early morning hours, he would bring the wagon down the hilly road and Marv told me they could always hear him coming. The jars of moonshine would rattle against each other, and in front of the wagon, Phoebe would be walking carrying a lantern so Jim could see. They would go down to the mouth of the valley, where the bridge is now, wait for a truck to come by and pick up the moonshine, and then they would come back up the road just as the sun was coming up. About every two months, Jim would go into Carter to pick up supplies and Phoebe would come back home alone. Sometimes she would stop here at the house and visit with Marv. He told me she always asked for me. She couldn't understand why I no longer lived here at the house. She seemed to realize I was trying to help her and in her feeble way, wanted to thank me.

I remember visiting with Marv one night when there was a revival being held at the schoolhouse. We walked up there and I could see Phoebe and Jim standing out by a window watching the people inside. I don't recall them ever talking with anyone around here. And people left them alone also. Jim put up a gate at the road to their house and never allowed anyone to open it. That road is up there by the cemetery. Up from the cemetery a little way, you can see a path leading up the hill. If you follow that for a mile or so, you will find their old house, or what's left of it, and the little cemetery where most of their family are buried. The last time I was up there, it had been cleaned up and there were markers at the graves.

Hubert died about the time Phoebe was twenty. He had a garden plot out back of the house and Ida had tried to raise some vegetables to help with the food supplies. Jim also liked to raise things and in addition to his corn for the moonshine, he would always grow a big crop of tomatoes. At every reunion I can remember, Jim would come down the little road on his horse with a big bag of tomatoes across the horse's back. He would dump them on the ground up by the school door and anyone who wanted tomatoes, could take what they wanted. He would then go and stand by the corner of the school and when most of the people had eaten what they wanted, he would get a paper plate and fill it up and go back to the corner to eat. Before he left, he would fill up another plate, and I suppose, take it back to Phoebe. Whenever I was there, he would always come over to me and say, 'Uncle Doug!" I would say back, 'Jim.'

That was all. He would speak to no one else other than to nod his head. Sometimes he would say to me that Phoebe said hello.

One year, on a particular hot day at the homecoming, we were about through eating and Jim was not anywhere around. Some of the women wondered where he was and one of the men laughed and said, 'I 'spect that Jim got his beard cut off and was so light headed he floated right away.' Some of the people snickered, but just then, here came Jim. His long gray beard was a sight to behold and people turned their heads to hide their grins.

Jim got off his horse, laid the tomatoes on the ground and came right over to me.

"Uncle Doug, Phoebe ain't well. She's been askin' fer ye fer a few days now. I tol' her I would get ye as soon as ye got hyar. Kin ye cum ta se her? She's poorly."

"Sure, Jim. I'll go with you. There's a cousin of yours here today who's a nurse. Would you like for me to bring her along? Maybe she can help Phoebe out."

"Whutever ye say, Uncle Doug! Whutever! Phoebe ain't well."

I asked Olivia, a registered nurse, and a cousin of Hubert's, if she would go with me to see Phoebe. Olivia was one of the few, maybe the only one, of Hubert's family, that people liked. We had to walk up the wagon trail and the heat was somewhat abated there in the shade of the trees. It was still pretty hot though.

When we got to the house, if you could call it a house, we found Phoebe lying outside under a large oak tree on some blankets Jim had put down for her. I'll admit it was cleaner out there than it was in the shack they called a house and it was also cooler. Olivia looked at her, then back at me, and shook her head. It was easy to see Phoebe had very little time left. She had had a baby and was bleeding slowly but steadily. The baby was born dead which was a blessing since it had to have been fathered by her brother, Jim. Jim had buried it over next to Ida. There were other graves there and I wondered whose they were. Jim had dug another grave next to the baby's. He knew that Phoebe was dying and had dug the grave for her. Over beside Hubert's grave, there was another spot dug out but it was nothing more than a large hole.

"Uncle Doug, thet's the third baby she's had and all of them died. I don't rikken I know whut went wrong. She jest had sumpthin' wrong with her, I guess."

There was no use to tell Jim what was wrong. He wouldn't understand it anyway and Phoebe was too feeble minded to know either. All Jim seemed to know these days was moonshining and tomatoes.

Phoebe died soon after we arrived and Jim just picked her up, put her in the grave he had dug and began filling the dirt over her. I started to object but Olivia placed her hand over mine and shook her head.

"It won't do any good, Uncle Doug. He thinks he's doing the right thing."

"Goodbye, Jim."

We left then, walking slowly down the hillside, each with our own thoughts. When we got to the bottom of the hill, we turned as we heard a gunshot coming from up at Jim's place. Some others heard it also, and thinking it might be us in trouble, came running toward the gate to the road. When they realized we were fine, they asked what had happened.

Looking over at some of the young men standing around the school, I said to them, "Boys, I think some of you had best go up to Jim's place to see what that shot was about. Be very careful because he doesn't like people around there."

Five or six of the men went up the path and sometime later, they came back and told me Jim had evidently shot himself in the head. They found him down in the hole by Hubert's grave.

One of the boys said it appeared he had climbed down in the hole and shot himself.

They had filled in the hole with the dirt Jim had dug.

That's about it, Ken. I have a lot of fond memories of this valley. Some say it's a hard life to live here, but back when I was young, we had church services, pie suppers, square dances and always a supply of Jim's 'shine. We may have had it hard but we didn't know it."

*****

Complete darkness had fallen. Up the valley, the whippoorwill again sang out. The owl was still hooting in the barn. The frogs sang their songs and the fireflies lit the blackness of the night. The last lantern in the house was extinguished and the stars twinkled in the dark sky. An old man looked out his window and once again rode his stick horse across the plains and over the hills—Then a tear fell!

EARLY SUNRISE

Farm built muscles exploded from the tattered clothes of the young man of sixteen, soon to be seventeen years. Stretching in relief, he wiped the perspiration from his forehead and opened his shirt, which was plastered to his body. Looking back on the plowed field he had just finished, he was proud of the long, straight furrows, and now his day was done and next week, he and Lark, could begin the spring corn planting.

Wiping again at his face, he reached for the bridles on the horses, and after he brushed down their sweat-covered bodies, he released them to run in the field. He removed his shirt and let the soft afternoon breeze help cool him off. From the waist up, his muscles fairly rippled. Over six feet tall and weighing about two hundred pounds, this young farm lad, Tom Perry, had set young ladies hearts aflutter here on McGlone Creek. He had curly black hair with deep dark eyes, which would stare right through you, and his always comfortable smile captured many a second glance from the local ladies.

Charlie, his older brother, was helping with the plowing today but next week he had to go to the County Seat to serve on jury duty for a week. Lark, the next oldest, would be here to help Tom Perry with the farm work while Charlie was away.

Tom Perry walked over to the next field where Charlie was finishing plowing.

"Whoa, boys! Whoa now!"

Beads of sweat dripped from Charlie's face as he stopped the two mules, removed his flour sack head covering, and swiped at the sweat bees buzzing around his head. These were mean little critters and would sting right through your clothing if you let them get on you.

Charlie called over to Tom, "You're all finished for the day? I have one more row to do and then I'll join you. I saw a big rattler down by the creek. It gave off some rattles and ol' Johnnie here wanted to stomp it but I pulled him back. That's the first rattler I've seen for some time. Hope it doesn't mean there are a lot around this year. I'll be with you in a jiffy."

Tom Perry had begun his plowing in the shrouded mists of the morning to take advantage of the coolness of the early morning breezes. It had been hot this past week, unseasonably hot for early spring, and as he and Charlie stood there in the early afternoon heat, he was glad he had started early. Charlie had not been far behind and Tom had teased him about being late. "For an old married man, I can't understand why you were late! I was beginning to believe you wouldn't get here until noon."

As Charlie walked away with the two mules, he called back to Tom, "I'm going to clean up and take the buggy into Carter. I'll be back before dark. Would you mind getting the buggy ready for me? Lark should be here before I leave next week and we can discuss what else needs to be done." Tom watched him walk away with adoration in his eyes. He had been close to Charlie, closer to him than to Lark, or to Carrie Lee, his sister.

Lark had not been around the farm much, having lived with his aunt in Grayson so he could attend school there. Lark and Tom had finished the sixth grade here on the Creek in the little schoolhouse their father, Andrew, had built. If they chose to go on to school, they had to go to Carter. Charlie wanted to quit school and Sarah insisted he continue, which caused Charlie to rebel so he decided to leave the farm and do some traveling. Lark went to Grayson to do his high school work, then made a decision to go and study the Bible to become a minister, and Tom finished the eighth grade. Carrie Lee had also finished the eighth grade and then went on to take two years of normal school, which was the same as high school.

One late summer day, Charlie had returned from his travels and brought with him, a beautiful young lady, who, he told Sarah, had agreed to be his wife. Since Charlie and Jessie weren't married when they arrived on the Creek, Charlie had to be careful around Sarah. She made arrangements for Jessie to live with Donna and her husband, Rick, up the valley a mile or so. "You two better arrange your wedding if you want to live together. Charles, it's sinful to live with that woman and not be married. I won't allow it."

"I know, Ma. We will get married as soon as plans can be made. How about a week from Sunday after services?"

"That'll be fine, Charles. I'll invite our friends and we'll have the preacher come out from Carter to do the service."

They all walked up to Donna's and she and Rick said they would be happy to keep Jessie until the wedding. She could help with the two children, Becky and Billy, and maybe she could help with some of the household chores while she was there.

Charlie had quite a story to tell about Jessie and how they had met. One evening while they were sitting around the kitchen table, Charlie told the family the story.

"I was standing on the pier in Philadelphia watching this big ship come in. I had been told it carried a bunch of ladies from Ireland who had come to America to find a better life. Since I was there looking for a wife, I thought this might be a good place to start. I saw all these women getting off the ship, scared and confused, and watched as a lady dressed as a nun, or so one of the men said, approached them. I moved up closer to hear what she was saying and I spotted this pretty little red haired girl and I fell for her right then and there. This nun told the girls her name was Sister Patricia and she could find work for some of them if they were interested.

I heard her say, 'There's a fine gentleman out in Berk County who is looking for a cook and a housekeeper. You'll have to work for him for one year for room and board, and remember, if you don't have work, the authorities may send you back to Ireland. All you have to do is sign these papers and I'll take you to him.'

There was a mad scramble among the girls and the Sister picked out four of them and said she would take two of the four with her. She would interview them after she had offered jobs to some of the others.

After she had finished with the others, some took her jobs and some didn't. She walked back to the four she had left standing near me. I was really taken by the red haired girl and I watched as Sister Patricia picked her to go with one of the others. She took the two of them over to a buggy being driven by a black man and told him to take the girls to the Sullivan farm.

When the girls turned to pick up their bags, I spoke with the black man, who said his name was Memphis.

'Memphis, where is this Sullivan farm? I may want to apply for a job there myself. Should I talk to the Sister?' I was using the job-hunting as an excuse to stay near the red-haired girl.

He looked at me with a funny look on his face and as he drove off, he said, 'Man, that warn't no nun. Is thet whut she tol' these wimmen folk? She be aworkin' the docks gettin' young'n's like these two to work fer people like 'at Mr. Sullivan. She gets paid to do thet.'

I ran after the buggy and asked Memphis if I could ride out to the farm with him.

'Climb 'yosef aboard. Ain't no reason one more cain't go wif us.'

Memphis went on with his talk. 'You know Mister, you cain't interfere with Mr. Sullivan now. He's a mean 'un all right and he gets a lot of these young'n's out to his farm. I don't know fer sure, but I do believe he has things in mind other than housekeeping and cooking fer these two. They sure be a pretty twosome.' He laughed as he drove on.

The longer I looked at the redhead, I was more certain I wanted her to be my wife. And she began to notice I was watching her and she kept smiling at me. It was a two day wagon ride to the Sullivan farm and that night, we camped out along a small stream with ol' Memphis giving me a stern warning to stay away from the ladies. 'Mr. Sullivan don't take kindly to any man lookin' at his wimmen folk. You jest stay here wif me and maybe, just maybe, he'll give you a job.'

It began to rain along about midnight and as Memphis hurried to the wagon to get a tarp to cover us, I motioned to the red head to come over to me. She moved over close and I said, 'Let's you and me get away from here. I can take you home with me and we'll get married and you'll have a wonderful life.'

Well, we left Memphis and the other girl without a goodbye, and headed straight west, staying away from most everybody. I had me a little money and we stopped to buy some food, but kept moving in case Memphis's Mr. Sullivan would try to find us. Late one afternoon, about five days after we left what was called Berk County, it began to rain again, and very hard this time. We spied a barn nearby, and decided to take shelter there and we slept that night in the hayloft, intending to be up and gone before anyone in the house awoke. When we did wake up, it was because a man was standing over us with a pitchfork in my face.

'As I live and breathe, I'm not accustomed to finding people asleep in my barn. 'Spect you best tell me who you are and why you're here.'

I told him our story and looking me over carefully, he said he believed me. He told me, 'Boy, I've heard of others like that Sullivan. Best you move on now because he's sure to have the law on you. Come over to the house and ma'll give you some biscuits, but you can't stay here. We don't want to get into any trouble.'

We left with a bag full of freshly baked biscuits and best wishes from the farmer and his wife. We caught a boat down the Ohio to Limestone, and we found a wagon of supplies coming this way.

That's how we met and we planned to get married when we arrived back here at home."

Pa wasn't too happy with him when he heard the story, but said, "Charles, what's done is done! I don't think much of what you did, but it's your life and you better hope that man can't find you."

"He won't find us out here, Pa. I doubt if he's even looking anymore.

When Jessie arrived she had very few clothes so Ma got busy and sewed her some dresses, mostly out of flour sacks she had stored away in the attic.

*****

Why ain't ya goin' ta church with us, Aunt Jessie?"

"Well, Becky, this is a special day..................."

"She's gettin' married, that's why. Billy yelled at her as he ran out the door. She ain't gonna' ta sleep with you no more. She's got her a man ta sleep with."

"Billy, you shut your mouth before I take a willow switch to you." Donna yelled at him as she chased him off the porch.

Donna came back into the house, took Becky's hand, and left with Billy and Becky for church, along with Rick.

As she left, she told Jessie, "Now, honey, if there's anything I can do to help you, just tell me. If you want to know anything about men, I can help you with that too. Lord knows, I've had enough experience. I guess it's a little late for that though."

There was to be a picnic after the wedding and as Charlie and Jessie were riding to the church in his buggy, Jessie whispered to him, "You're a good man, Charlie, and I'm glad you asked me to marry you. I'll do my best to make you a good wife."

Charlie had stopped at Donna's the night before presumably to bring Rick and Donna some eggs and butter. Rick and Donna sat with them on the porch listening to the sounds of the night, and shortly, Rick took a lantern and said he had to go to the barn to

67

check on the horses, and Donna said she had to clean up the house. Charlie reached for Jessie, held her close, kissed her, and left for home. As he walked away, he called back, "I love you, Jessie."

"Here she comes! Here comes the bride!" Yells came from the church and Becky ran to Jessie and grabbed her by the hand, and walked beside the slowly moving buggy.

"You'll come back and see me, won't you, Aunt Jessie?"

"Yes, dear. We'll live here and Aunt Jessie will always come see you, and someday you'll be a big girl and can find a handsome man and get married. You just be a good girl and do what your momma says."

As the buggy stopped, Charlie hurried around to her side and gave her a hand, and a big hug, to the cheers of the families gathered there.

Charlie and Jessie stood there as the heavily perspiring preacher approached. He wiped his brow, "If the bride and groom are ready, we are ready for this blessed event to begin. If you will just come this way."

The people gathered again in the church building. One of the ladies sang a shrill solo, and the ceremony began.

"Miss Jessie, will you take this man, Charlie, to be thy lawful wedded..."

"I will." Jessie replied before the preacher could finish the sentence. She was ready for the preacher to stop his droning and to get on with the ceremony.

It was a hot, humid Sunday afternoon, the circuit-riding preacher had given a long sermon that morning and the people were getting restless. The afternoon had heated up the tin roofed building and most of the women were using fans. Jessie was beginning to feel the sweat creep down her back.

"Yes sir, Mr. Preacher man, I surely will." She turned and smiled at Charlie.

"................I now pronounce you man and wife." The ceremony was over. Folks wished the newly married couple good luck, went to the picnic tables and ate. Very soon, everyone left for their homes to tend to the evening chores. A wedding was cause for celebration in the valley but they also had to think of the evening chores, which had to be finished before dark, and some of them had come several miles for the wedding.

*****

Tom Perry got the buggy ready and then walked down along the creek bank to where a trickling stream meandered down hill through a wild brushy spot. He always went here when he wanted to be alone. He had discovered this little hideaway when he was about ten years old and it had always been, in his eyes, his! This spot was up past the field into a dark, tree lined area where, as far as he knew, no one else had been, or at least, hadn't been as far back as he could remember. Tom had long ago made a small dam of stone and tree branches so there was a little pool of clear, cold water not far from where the water came out of the ground from the spring. He sat and watched the little ripples of water as they played over the stones he had placed in the pool. There was a bed of moss, which he sometimes lay on and watched the lazy clouds creep across the sky. In the early spring, the tree branches were like skeletons waving in the constant breeze. Later, as the leaves began to develop, it became a canopy of beauty, where the birds came to sing and to nest. He was tired today as he came to his 'spot,' and he lay down and soon dropped off to sleep.

He awoke with a start!

"Jessie! What are you doing? Get your hands out of my britches! You put that dress back on right now or I'll tell Charlie what you're doing and he'll make you walk all the way back to Pennsylvania. Go on now! You best do as I say!

A tiny breeze blew across the pool and a ripple played tag with a leaf. White clouds moved across the sky and the first blossoms of redbud had appeared. It was a perfect spring day. At least it was until Jessie showed up.

"Tom Perry, don'cha be like all them other young fellers. You boys all laugh and talk about how you want it and then you're all afraid of it when it's there. C'mon Tom Perry. Let little Jessie show you how it is to be loved."

Tom looked at the nearly unclothed young woman and couldn't help but wonder what pleasures she could show him. "Go on now, woman. Do as I say. Don't you ever forget you're married to my brother, Charlie, and I don't take kindly to how you're acting."

Jessie, pouting, picked up her flour sack dress and wrapped it around her. She had been rounding up some cows, which had strayed off into a wild onion patch, and had seen Tom walk up alongside the creek bank. She had followed and watched him from a clump of bushes just across the spring. She knew Charlie had gone to Carter and a big smile came to her face as she carefully walked over to where Tom was napping. Quietly slipping up on him, she had quietly dropped her dress to the ground.

"You're a 'fraidy cat, Tom Perry. You're a 'fraidy cat." She muttered out loud as she dressed. "Fraidy cat, Tom! 'Fraidy cat, Tom!" She sang as she walked out into the field heading toward the barn.

"Whew! I guess this place isn't as secret as I supposed." Tom remarked to himself. He stripped off his clothes and sat down in 'his' little pool of water to cool off.

Calming down, he recalled Charlie bringing Jessie home from Pennsylvania about three years ago. She was about three years older than Tom and she surely was a pretty thing.

While Tom sat in the water remembering how Jessie looked as she took off her dress, he remembered the day she and Charlie got married. Ma had made her a dress. She was a beautiful woman, with her red hair streaming down her back and some freckles on her nose and cheeks. When they left the church building, some of the younger kids had teased them with a little song, which Ma had taught them. "Going up McGlone Creek, going in a whirl. Going up McGlone Creek to get hissef' a girl. Wedding on McGlone Creek, very well known. Good lookin' Jessie and Charlie McGlone.

*****

Tom Perry laughed as he remembered those days. Standing up, he dried himself with his old flour sack shirt, carefully looking around to see if Jessie might be hiding in the bushes.

He sat back down on the moss-covered ground and remembered the days since Jessie had arrived.

When Tom Perry was about sixteen, Jessie had begun to pester him. She would show up in places where he was working alone and would tease him about his size and how she could make him enjoy work even more. Charlie never seemed to notice and Tom did his best to stay away from her. However, she was getting more and more desirable to him but he always remembered Charlie, and nothing happened except in his thoughts. As he dressed, he muttered to himself, "That woman is going to get herself into big trouble someday but not with me, she isn't."

*****

One extremely hot day, Andrew had been working out in the fields hoping to get some tree stumps moved so he could plow more land next summer. Tom and Charlie had wanted to help but he told them to take the day off after they got the corn planted. "Why don't you take the day off and go hunting? I believe we could use some fresh rabbit meat, but I doubt if you boys can find any. Probably couldn't hit one of them if you saw it!" They all laughed since the three of them were excellent shots.

Andrew was not a tall man but he was wide in the shoulders and was as strong as any man could be at his size. Tom was a lot like Andrew, except he was taller and weighed a little more. Both Tom and Andrew were very emotional and when anyone was hurt, they would both `hurt' with them.

When Tom was little and Andrew was out plowing the fields, he would let Tom follow behind and as the plow broke the dirt clods, Tom would step in them and laugh at the dirt oozing up between his toes. Sometimes he would step on a stone or a bee would sting him and he would cry a little. "Now Tom Perry, cryin' don't help a'tall so just be right careful where you step." Andrew would walk over to Tom , wipe away the tears, smile, and then Tom Perry would continue to follow behind the plow.

Later that afternoon, Lark had arrived with Nancy Susan, his wife to be, and Charlie went out to the field where Andrew was working to tell him they had arrived.

Andrew stopped his work on the stumps and went with Charlie back to the house. As they let out the mules on the way back, Andrew felt some pain, but said nothing to Charlie. It had been a hot muggy day and Andrew had been perspiring a lot and as they arrived at the house, Charlie went to the well to get some cold water to drink and Andrew started up the porch steps. As he reached the top step, he looked over at Lark, smiled, grabbed his chest and fell to the ground. Lark grabbed for him but Andrew was dead with a heart attack before they could get to him.

That evening, the family was seated around the supper table where two of the neighbors had just served them a big meal. The three brothers were there along with Jessie and Nancy Susan and Sarah.   Sitting next to Tom Perry , Jessie kept rubbing her leg up against his under the table. Tom was nervous and kept looking at Charlie who, at Sarah's request, was now sitting at the head of the table. She had told him that pa would want it that way. Lark, sitting across from Tom, lit up his pipe. He was concerned that Tom was choked up and almost in tears. Lark sat there quietly for a few minutes, glancing at both Tom and Jessie as though he suspected something.

He tapped out the tobacco in his pipe, looked over at Tom, and quietly said, "We all know pa put in a good life but a hard one. I'll miss him. I know all of you will. I believe you, Tom, will miss him most of all since you and pa were very close. But we have to try and understand that pa was just tired and couldn't go on. Sometimes I think he knew he didn't have long to live. We'll all grieve, but remember, he did leave us some good memories."

This was a good family, close to each other, yet letting each grow in his or her own way. Charlie was seemingly the head of the family now that Andrew was gone. Sarah wanted it that way.

Nancy Susan got up from the table to help clear away the dishes and Jessie said she would help. As she started to get up, she reached down like she was getting something from the floor, grabbed Tom's leg and rubbed her hand up it.

After the girls cleaned the table and left the room, Charlie got Andrew's will from the family Bible. Sarah had written out the will about a year before he died and had put it between the pages of the Old and New Testament.

Sarah could read and write so she had kept the family history in her Bible.

She had helped Tom with his schooling and he could read and write pretty well, something Charlie couldn't do, at least not much. Tom had been interested in learning about reading so she taught him from the Bible, the only book she had brought with her from Virginia. Charlie learned what little he knew from listening to her and Tom and from his four years of going to school. Much later, when Tom started to school, he already could read some things.

Sarah had left the room to be with the girls. She knew what was in the will and wanted the boys to be alone for a while.

As Charlie held the Bible, he spoke to Tom Perry and Lark, "Remember what a strict believer Ma is in the Bible? I remember how she would try to teach it to me but I guess I wasn't good at learning. In the evenings she would sit on the porch swing and read it to me and try to explain what it meant, but I never did fully understand."

Tom and Lark said they remembered.

Charlie moved over to Lark, handed him the Bible and told him he would have to read the will since he was going to be a preacher and knew about such things.

Lark pulled out the will from between the pages and read the paper with tears in his eyes.

He read. "I, Andrew McGlone, give all my land I have cleared here in this valley to Charles and Thomas Perry. The boys are to get equal shares of the land if they stay here and farm it. Larkin knows about this and has agreed that he doesn't want any part of the farm. If one of them don't stay, then the one who does stay is to buy at a fair price, the other's share. Carrie Lee has married and has her own family to care for her. I love you all. I shorly do!"

Down at the bottom of the page, it was signed simply, "Yore Pa."

Lark handed the will to Charlie and walked out to the porch and sat in the swing. The night creatures were beginning their singing as the shadows of darkness began to spread over McGlone Creek. Lark cried for a few minutes, then looked up as the others joined him on the porch. "Listen to those whippoorwills. Pa always liked to listen to the whippoorwills. Claimed they would bring good luck as long as they sang."

Charlie tried to change the subject. "Remember when we would go down to the swimmin' hole and watch the neighbor girls take their bath? I remember once we were hiding the in the bushes, thinking no one could see us, and ma came up behind us with a willow switch and got a lick in on all of us. I even remember what she said. 'Nary a one of you are gonna get a bite to eat tonight and I'm agoin' to tell your pa he needs to keep you busy in the fields. Now get out there and help him.'"

Chuckling, he went on. "'Yessum, Ma,' we'd say, and the next chance we got, we'd be right back there in the bushes!"

They laughed and that started a session of memories among the three of them.

Charlie spoke up. "I can see ma standing there before the fireplace with pa sitting over there in his rocker, and she would say to us, 'It's time for you boys to go to bed now.' Pa would look over at us, give us a wink, and say, 'Before you go to bed, you boys remember you need to feed the hogs and chickens tomorrow because I'm going to be busy. And while you're at it, help your ma bring in the eggs.'"

Time passed quickly that evening. They had decided to bury Andrew the next day over in the little cemetery across from the church. One of the neighbors was making a wooden casket for Andrew and said it would be finished by afternoon tomorrow. Services were to be held in the church house Andrew had built up the road from the home place. Arrangements would be made by one of the neighbors to have a preacher from Carter come and hold the services.

Sarah had gone to her bedroom to grieve in her own way. She was strong and was handling this quite well. "There's a time for grievin' and a time to be strong. My family needs me and I know pa would understand. I'll grieve when the time comes for me to."

The family talked awhile longer and Charlie said the thought he would turn in. "It's been a long day for me." He got up and walked into the house. Tom Perry and Lark decided to take a walk and Nancy Susan and Jessie asked to come along. "Fine with me," said Charlie as he closed the door. "I doubt if those two will want a couple of women bothering them however."

The four of them walked along the path to the church with Tom carrying a lantern. Nothing was said by the two boys, and the girls, coming up behind, tried to keep still. Tom stopped in the path, looked out into the darkness, "Lark, wonder what it was like back then? Back when ma and pa first came to the valley? Pa said he could farm about fifty acres when he first came here and now he has cleared almost two hundred acres. He certainly was a worker!" His voice was about to break so Lark put his hand on his arm as they walked on.

"He had quite a story to tell us about bringing the mules on the boat. I can see him now settling back in the rocker, lighting up his pipe, and telling us the stories. You and Charlie got bored with him telling the tales, but not me, no, sir. I enjoyed them every time he told them." Tom Perry spoke softly to Lark and both now had tears on their cheeks.

Over in the barn, one of the mules gave out a loud bray. Jessie had left Tom alone, but now she walked up to him and rubbed herself against him as they walked over to see what was wrong with the mules. Lark and Nancy Susan walked on toward the house so they could be alone. That left Tom alone with Jessie and that made him very uncomfortable. In spite of his turning the lantern light up as high as it would go, she rubbed her hand over him, and he, being a healthy young man, felt himself being aroused.

The mules in the barn were fine. The wind had picked up and was blowing through the cedars along the road. Tom often dreamed of going off with the winds as they blew over the hills. Jessie had suggested they go up in the hayloft but Tom again thought of Charlie, and told her no. She pouted and tried to get him to hold her but he wouldn't do that either. As they left the barn and walked back toward the house, the moon peeked out from behind the clouds and Tom was mightily tempted to take Jessie in his arms, but he just couldn't do it.

"Smell that honeysuckle, Tom Perry? Little Jessie can smell a lot better than that. Just hold me and kiss me. You'll like it, big man. You'll like it."

Tom pushed her away, walked her up to the porch steps and left her there. He went around behind the house to a big cedar tree standing on the nearby hill. He sat there under the tree looking out over the moonlit valley.   As he sat there, he remembered again how he sat at Andrew's side as he listened to the tales of adventure. He and Charlie would laugh at the stories. Sometimes he would get up and walk around the room pretending to be a great explorer, and Andrew, watching him, would smile, sit back and smoke his corncob pipe. Soon his eyes would close and he would drift off to sleep. Sarah would shake Andrew awake and tell him to get ready for bed. "Pa," she'd say, "You quit telling stories to them boys. You sure enough are going to have them scared to death." Andrew would laugh, say, "Goodnight, boys," and go off to bed.

Tom heard Jim and Nancy Susan go to the house. He leaned back against the tree and fell asleep.

Suddenly he was awakened! He jumped up and Jessie grabbed him and kissed him hard. "Tom Perry, you're not 'agoin to get away from me this time. I want you and I intend to have you."

Too startled to react, he fell to the ground with Jessie on top of him. She was kissing him and tearing at his clothes but he pushed her off and took off running for the house. He fell over a rain barrel on his way down the hill, but it didn't seem to wake anyone so he tiptoed into the house and went off to his room. Some time later, he heard Jessie come in.

Still shaking, he fell off to sleep.

*****

Sarah seemed to have lost her spirit. She used to go out in the fields in the early morning, while the dew was still on the grass, and pick some tender dandelions to make a dandelion salad. Now, she would send one of the boys out, or not get them at all. And this was her favorite salad! She would always pick a fresh bouquet of flowers each morning, but no longer. What she did pick, stayed in the vases too long, and withered. No longer did she wander out to the garden to see if the vegetables were ready to be picked, or if they were doing well. She would come to the kitchen in the morning and sometimes forget to light the fire, and the boys had to wait for breakfast. No longer was there singing in the house; no longer was there laughter.

A few months after Andrew died, she became ill and stayed in bed while the men folk went about their work. Tom gathered the eggs and did some of the other work Sarah usually did. He caught a chicken, wrung its neck and flipped it, still moving, over on the grass until it stopped jerking.   They were planning to have chicken and dumplings that night and Nancy Susan was going to fix supper. He then went into the house to see how Sarah was and would always remember her saying to him. "I've tried to teach you boys to talk right, Tom Perry. Not like your poor ol' Ma, but right, like people with learning do. I rikken I do talk a bit funny 'cause 'o habit and I can't rightly hep it, but read them books Tom Perry , read and learn. Learn to be right proper. Do me a favor, boy, be a proper gentleman."

"I'll try Ma, I'll try." Tom began sobbing, as his ma just closed her eyes and died.

After they buried her, he went up into the hills and stayed most of two days before going home. Wilderness living in Kentucky was hard on all of them, but particularly hard on Sarah. Though strong in spirit, she was not a big woman. She struggled to raise her family and help with the farm chores until finally, the heart went out of her when she lost her Andrew and she didn't want to go on.

Charlie had waited as long as he could for Lark to show up but he was going to be late reporting for jury duty if he didn't leave right away.

"Jessie, I may pass him on the way in to Grayson but in case I miss him, tell him to make sure the cattle back on Punkin' Meadow are looked after. And tell him that Tom Perry will do the plowing, or what's left to do. By the way, where is Tom ?"

"I don't know, Charlie. He was going hunting the last I saw of him. Maybe he hasn't come back. He'll probably sleep over at Rick and Donna's tonight. Said he was going to hunt up that way. If he comes back tonight, I'll tell him what you said.   I'm sure you'll probably pass Lark on the road, since that's the only road there is! Don't you worry about a thing. I can handle the household chores and I'll do the milking and gather the eggs. The boys can do the rest. You have a good time and don't be too hard on the other jurors." Jessie laughed with Charlie, kissed him on the cheek, and as he rode away, she waved at him and went back into the house.

Later that evening, the McCarty's from up on Punkin' Meadows, came by in their wagon, stopped in for a drink of water and spent some time visiting with Jessie. They had passed Charlie on the road but had not seen Lark. They had their niece with them and she had strong feelings for Tom Perry but he had ignored her. The girl had asked Jessie where he was and she replied she hadn't seen him all day. Wanting to make the girl jealous, Jessie said he might be over at Wesleyville visiting a young girl he knew there.

"It'll be getting dark soon, Jessie. Best we be gettin' on home. If we can be of any help while Charlie is away, you just call on us." Climbing into the wagon, the McCarty's rode away and Jessie walked up on the porch and sat in the swing and watched over the valley as an almost full moon was rising above the hills and shining through the apple tree branches. The birds were settling in for the night and there was a soft breeze wafting across the trees and the aroma of the honeysuckle was strong upon the wind. In the nearby hills the whippoorwills were starting their singing and along with the frogs down in the creek, the valley was sending its music across the winds. The moon began to cause the stars to fade away.

Tom Perry came up the little dirt road, walked over to the well to get a drink, and came up on the porch to sit.

"Where's Lark? I thought I saw his buggy here a few minutes ago. Did Nancy Susan come with him?"

Jessie still sat in the swing as Tom moved over to the porch banister to sit. "That was the McCarty's and their niece. I haven't heard from Lark. Charlie said he would probably meet him on the road somewhere. He told me what to tell Lark, and he said for you to finish up the plowing, or what there was left to do. He wanted Lark to check on the cattle up on the ridge but you may have to do that. Have you been hunting?"

"No. I just wanted to be alone for a while. I'm sorry to have missed Charlie. Did he get away in time?"

"He said he would be fine. Would you like a glass of lemonade? I made some up fresh and sent a bottle with Charlie along with some sandwiches."

They sat there, Jessie in the swing and Tom Perry on the porch railing. Jessie had brought two glasses of lemonade, and as they sat there, the moon filled the valley with light. Tom Perry finally said he would go down and check the barn. One of the hogs was having some trouble and he wanted to check on it. They had a two-day-old calf and he also wanted to see if things were all right with it and its mother.

"Do you want me to go with you? I don't think you'll need a lantern with this bright moon."

"No, I'll be fine. In fact, I think I'll just sleep down there. Tell Lark I'll see him early in the morning."

Tom Perry was not comfortable sleeping in the house with Jessie and no one else there. He didn't say that to her but both of them knew the reason.

Next day, early morning, as Jessie was gathering the eggs and Tom Perry was doing the milking, she said to him, "Could it be that little Tom Perry was afraid of Jessie last night? You didn't need to sleep in the barn because of me." Laughing at his discomfort, she took the eggs to the house, calling back at him, "Breakfast will be ready soon. Don't be long."

Farm work kept Tom busy next day and as he rode his horse down from Punkin' Meadow, he thought he would have Lark go back up there later in the week to check the cattle. They were all right now but some were ready to calve and they should be looked after. While up there he had relived some of his youth with vivid imaginings.

Finding Lark still not there, he was a little worried about him. "Maybe I should ride down toward Carter and see if anyone has seen him. It isn't like Lark not to show up. If he isn't here by noon tomorrow, I'll go into Grayson to see if he's all right."

Jessie had prepared a big supper, thinking Lark and Nancy Susan would be there. It was rather warm so she and Tom Perry decided to eat out on the porch. "If there was anything wrong, Charlie would have let us know. I think something has happened to cause him to be a few days late but I'm sure he will be here." Jessie walked over to Tom Perry and placed her hand on his shoulder, knowing he was concerned, and tried to assure him all was well.

They again sat on the porch that evening and watched the bats swarms around catching the night insects. The mosquitoes were not too bad this year and the evenings spent outside were very pleasant. The farmhouse was whitewashed and in the bright moonlight, it stood out in a ghostly silence. Jessie had not lit the lanterns so the only light they had was the moonlight. Earlier that day, Tom Perry had told her he thought it was going to rain.

"I think you're wrong, Tom Perry. It doesn't look like rain to me."

"Look out over those hills. See those clouds beginning to roll in? "

Shortly, in the darkening sky, there was a distant rumble of thunder and as they sat there on the porch listening to the beautiful sounds of the night creatures in the valley, the moon gradually disappeared into the darkness of the clouds. Tom Perry said he was going to the barn to check on the animals and Jessie went into the house to get some candles and to light some of the kerosene lamps.

"Tom Perry, you come back tonight, you hear? I'm scared of the thunder and lightning."

Tom wasn't going back to the house for anything and later that evening as the rain began as a sprinkle and later as a torrential downpour with lightning and thunder, someone crawling under the blanket with him, awakened him. Not quite awake, he stuttered something and rolled back over.

Then, waking with a start, he realized Jessie was beside him with nothing on and giving him kisses all over his body. He tried to come awake and push her away but she would have no part of it. As a great rumble of thunder sounded overhead, he succumbed to her and they made love for the rest of the night, over and over and over. Thoughts of what he was doing didn't enter his head and Jessie was always there urging him on for more and more. Finally, at daybreak, she rolled away, exhausted, saying she could take no more. She quickly pulled her dress on and saying nothing more, left him lying there on the blanket in the straw.

Shocked! Tom Perry greeted the morning in total shock. "What have I done?" Turning his head down into the blanket, he yelled out, "What have I done?" Not at all ashamed of crying, he wept great sobs. And yet, he felt as if he had experienced one of the great moments of his life. Spending little time in the barn, he dressed, left for the creek where he followed the stream to his hideaway. The morning moved on and as Tom Perry sat there in stunned silence, thinking what he had done to Charlie, he made his decision. "I have to leave and I have to leave now." Taking a bath in the cool water, he thought about what he was going to do.

Going back to the house, he stormed off to his room, took some of his clothes, his rifle, and in the kitchen he made some sandwiches, went to the barn to get his horse, and rode away.

As he rode down the little hill into Carter, he met Lark on his way to the farm. Trying hard not to be seen by Lark, he hid behind a large sycamore tree, but no use, Lark had seen him already. "Hi, Tom Perry. What are you doing down here? I'm sorry I'm late. Nancy Susan was not well and I felt I had best stay with her. Tie your horse to the buggy and ride back with me."

"I'm not going back, Lark. I can't! I just can't! Don't ask me why, but there is no way I can go back. This is goodbye, Lark. You tell Charlie goodbye for me.

Lark climbed down from his buggy and stood quietly as Tom Perry slid from his horse and said, "I need to go, Lark. I just think it's the right thing to do. I'll be all right. One of my friends said there is a lot of lumbering going on up in Michigan and I may go up there for a while. After that, I don't know. I may go to visit with Uncle Bill in Indiana. I have to go so don't try to talk me out of it. Lark, I loved my life here on the farm, and you and Charlie, and Carrie Lee. But I can't stay. Something awful has happened to me and I have to get away."

Tom Perry, crying now, walked over to Lark, wrapped his arms around him, and said he would probably never see him again. Mounting his horse, he rode away, not looking back, instead keeping his eyes roaming out across the valley, which had always been his home. Near the first bend in the road, he heard Lark call out a final goodbye!

DREAMS

Twilight grabbed the late evening sun and pulled it slowly toward the horizon. Great streaks of reds and yellows laced the clouds as dark shadows moved across the earth.

An elderly man with a slight stoop walked out of the barn, went over to the well, drew a bucket of water, and moved toward the house carrying the bucket. He watched in the distance as a car moved along the narrow paved road and turned into the dirt lane leading to the farmhouse. Dust rose up behind the car as it slowed down to enter the driveway to the house.

Three people got out of the car. A young man and a young lady were in the front seat and an older man sat in the back seat.

"Hey, Grandpa Roy."

The young man walked rapidly over to the old man who was now sitting on the porch, grabbed his hand with a hearty handshake and then wrapped him up with a hug.

"Grandpa, I want you to meet Miya. She says she is the cutest and sweetest girl I'll ever get to meet. Says she is too good for me but may condescend to be seen with me."

Blushing with a deep red, Miya shook hands and then she too, gave Grandpa Roy a hug.

"Don't listen to him, sir. He's always telling me how wonderful I am and I'm getting to almost believe him."

Laughing at them both, Grandpa stood back and looked Miya over. He turned to look at Greg.

"You know son, I agree with her. She is the cutest girl you'll ever meet and I 'spect she is also the sweetest. Miya, I'm sure glad to meet you. We've heard good things about you and now that I've seen you, I believe them all."

He put his arms around the two youngsters, and they walked over to the car where his son, Walter, was getting the baggage from the trunk.

"Good to see you, Dad."

Walter wrapped his father in his arms and smiled broadly.

"These two invited me along, although I don't know why. I guess it was time for me to visit with you and Faye. Hope you can put us up for a day or so."

"Sure we can. Come on in the house. Faye's at the store but she'll be back shortly."

Greg was a fine looking, tall, slender young man of twenty-three. Miya looked to be about the same age. She was stunning in her beauty and her face was a face of smiles. Long black hair cascaded down her back and her bluish-green eyes gave out the twinkle of enjoyment. Greg's father, Walter, was the older of two boys and was very close to his father. He lived several hundred miles away but got back to the farm as often as he could.

Walter and Greg put the luggage in their rooms, grabbed some of Faye's cookies from the kitchen, and walked back out on the porch where Grandpa Roy was sitting in the swing.

Roy waved down the road, "Here comes Faye now. She'll be glad to see you, Greg. Maybe she can teach you to cook because Miya is too pretty to be in the kitchen. I remember when Faye told me the same thing about herself. Trouble is, I was too stubborn to learn to cook, so she took her beauty into the kitchen and still has it."

Greetings were called to Faye as she walked out of the garage to greet them. Faye soon had supper cooking and Miya volunteered to help her.

"Miya, I forgot to get bananas at the store. I promised Roy I would make him a banana pudding tonight and I only have two bananas here. I'll have to go back. Can you keep an eye on things while I'm gone?"

Walking out to the porch, she asked Walter if he would like to ride along with her; Miya busied herself in the kitchen and that left Grandpa Roy and Greg to sit on the porch and talk.

"Grandpa, let's take a walk. I need to talk with someone and I think that someone should be you."

"Fine, Greg. Any place in particular you want to walk to?"

Let's walk down by the pond. I remember when you used to take me down there and we would fish from the bank. We never caught anything but pan fish. You would always say the big ones were out in the middle and you needed to get a boat to get out there. Did you ever get the boat?"

"No, I never got the boat. 'Spect I never will. I don't go fishing as much as I used to. I don't enjoy it much when I'm alone and Faye never cared for it. Maybe we can go while you're here. I know your dad would like to go with us. I believe there are a couple of rods in the garage."

Greg led the way. They stopped by the barn to see a new calf, which had just been born that morning and Greg climbed up the hayloft ladder to glance at the hay in the upper part of the barn.

"I used to play here a lot. Me and Ben would come up here and hide when dad was looking for us."

"My boy, I 'spect he knew where you were all the time. When he was a little fellow, he and his friends would come up here and hide from your grandma. She would pretend she didn't know where they were, all the time listening to their giggles. Not much got past your grandma. Not even when your dad would try to bring one of the little girls up here! I guess you're not supposed to know that, though."

Leaving the barn, they walked slowly down to the pond. Frogs were singing and Greg was deep in thought. Roy eyed him for awhile, then, lighting his pipe, "What's on your mind, boy?

It certainly isn't the memories of the barn, or the little calf. As we've walked along, you've talked about everything but what to ask me. I can tell. Have you got some kind of trouble?"

"I don't know, Grandpa. Maybe I shouldn't bother you. It may not be that important and I don't need to bother you with my problems."

"It's all right, son. You can ask me anything you want and I feel honored that you care enough to ask. Go ahead."

"I can't think of anything except Miya; when I'm not with her, I want to call her all the time. I can't wait to see her each day. And on days I don't see her, I really feel miserable. I just can't seem to function real well unless she is with me. Sometimes she tells me she likes to be alone for awhile. Then, when she says that, I feel real guilty."

Greg stammered with his words, but went on. "Her mother says we see too much of each other and tries to stop us sometimes. That makes me upset with her mother. I just want to be with Miya; that's all."

"Nothing wrong with that, Greg. However, you have to give her some space to be herself, to breathe on her own, but there's nothing wrong with wanting to be with her all the time. Sounds like a pretty strong case to me."

"We want to get married but her mother doesn't think we know each other well enough. We've gone together for over a year and we both think we know what we want. How do you know when you're in love? Maybe I should have asked dad, but I don't think he was in love with mom and I don't think she was in love with him. I really don't think her mother and stepfather care for me but Miya says that isn't so. She's in a quandary, trying to defend her mother, yet wanting to marry me. Do you mind my asking you this question?"

They walked over to a mossy spot near the creek, sat down, and watched the young calves play in a nearby meadow. Over on the side of the hill, Greg spotted a few deer and commented that he never remembered any deer around the farm before.

They're getting plentiful around here, Greg. I 'spect we'll have to start shooting some to keep them out of the corn. I never cared much about killing animals but maybe the deer are too plentiful. Some of the neighbors have already shot a few and I may have to do the same."

Grandpa stretched out against a sycamore tree and started to tell Greg a story.

"Whoops! There's the dinner bell. You may not want to hear my story, but if you do, we can continue after dinner."

"I would be delighted to hear your story, Grandpa."

"Maybe I'm the one who has a need to talk to someone. And, if you want, maybe Miya should listen. You think about it. I think it would be good for me to talk about it and maybe my thoughts will help both you and Miya to make a decision. Now let's go and finish off that meat loaf and get some of Faye's banana pudding. My, that's good stuff!"

With spryness in his step, Grandpa Roy walked past the barn, stopped to look in on the calves, and then he and Greg walked to the house.

After supper, Miya said she would help Faye with the dishes, but Walter said no, he would do it.

"I haven't seen Faye for a long time and I want to visit with her. Miya, you go along with Greg and Grandpa."

Miya went out to the porch with Greg, and Roy joined them after coming from the barn. He had his lantern with him since darkness was now almost complete. Over a nearby hill, the almost full moon showed promise of lighting up the sky.

"Won't need this lantern in another hour or so. That moon is going to be bright tonight." Roy walked over to the porch and sat down.

"You two listen to those sounds. Those are the sweetest sounds you can hear. The frogs are singing to us, the whippoorwills are really singing tonight, and hear that old barn owl? He has his eyes on something down in the barn." Roy stepped over to the porch rail, cleaned out his pipe, sat down in the swing, and was quiet for a little while.

"You realize you must make up your own minds about getting married. Greg is a fine young man and I'm very proud to be his grandfather. From what I've heard, Miya, you're a fine young lady. Greg asked me earlier what love is, and I'm not sure I know the answer. Your grandma didn't think I knew, Greg. But Faye knows. She's a lovely lady and I'm so fortunate to have her with me. You two sit right here in the swing and let me reminisce a bit and try to explain what love means to me. I'll sit over here in the rocker."

Grandpa Roy sat down in the rocker, rocking back and forth, and then almost in a whisper-------

"Now that I think back about it, I've been lucky. Very lucky! I've felt two loves. One is there in the kitchen and there is no finer woman than she is. She's exactly the one I always wanted to be with and I was blessed to meet her in a critical time of my life.

The other, well-----. The other came to me out of the early shadows of my life, out of the mists of another world. And she disappeared from me the same way, walking off into the deepening darkness of life.

When I was eighteen years old, I went away to college. That year was a time of renewal for mankind. The war was just over and many of the veterans were returning to school and here I was, a naïve young lad, mentally trying to compete with men who had faced death, who had fought for the freedom we all now enjoy, and wanted to learn and get on with their lives. I was trying. I was trying too hard!

One night I went to a party at a girls' dormitory and while there, met one of my buddy's friends. For some strange reason, we all called her 'mother,' and she told me she had a friend she wanted me to meet. As she introduced me to Dorothy, I gazed upon the most beautiful girl I had ever met. And that's still true to this day. The rest of the evening passed in a blur for me—I only knew that I was in a trance and having no idea what I may have said to her. I did get up enough nerve to ask her out the next night and she accepted!

I walked back to my room that night and I know my feet were off the ground! Some may call it walking on clouds and I guess I would have to agree with that.

Next evening as I went to call on her, I completely forgot her name and horrors upon horrors, what was I to do? All kinds of thoughts came to me and when I opened the door to her dormitory, there sat 'mother' at the desk. Well now! I was saved. She asked me if I was there for Dorothy and I said yes, secretly wiping away my fears.

Back in those days, we had to ask at the desk for them to call our dates for us. None of this going to their rooms or anything like that. I suppose you think we were old fashioned, and I guess to an extent, we were.

What happened from January to May of that year is now a blur. I remember I 'walked on those clouds' for a few months because her beauty, her down home kind of wit, and all around personality, would not let my feet touch the ground. Back then I felt those months were as years of happiness, love and joy. School was out in May; she went her way and I went mine. However, I did go visit her that summer and as time for parting came, I realized we would never again stroll hand in hand through my land of 'pretending' and as she slowly started to walk away, I reached for her in my dreams."

As Greg and Miya sat there, a slight breeze had sprung up and brushed away the sadness in Grandpa Roy's heart. The wind swept across the porch and Roy felt a deep loneliness in his weary heart. He walked over to the path leading to the front gate, and as the darkness moved away with the light of the moon, he looked into the star filled sky. He long ago had picked out a bright twinkling star as her star. He stepped back to the porch, sat in his rocker, and watched as a shooting star crossed the sky. A woodland quietness settled in over the farm, broken only by the singing of the night birds. Roy looked at Greg and Miya, smiled, and went on with his story.

"I left her then, knowing full well that I was in love with her. But you see, this was another kind of love. It was the love of a naïve young man who let emotions enter too quickly into his heart and this is what I want you two to be careful of. Each time you see a star in the sky, each time a bird flies past you, each time a flower blooms, you must feel love, a love for each other. Make yourselves part of the wonderful world God has created for us and never, never doubt that your spirit is a spirit of love—love for each other."

Greg looked at Miya. " Didn't know grandpa knew about such things. I wish I could speak to you like that."

Miya squeezed Greg's hand. "No, Greg. Those are words from his heart and they are his words. He's telling us to be sure of our love."

Roy sat there as the great moon rose higher over the valley. Soon, he walked over to Greg and Miya, held their hands and said, "Excuse me, you two. I guess I got carried away with my thoughts. You asked me what love is? I don't know! I think it is a feeling one has within oneself—a feeling to share with another. I know I have that feeling for Faye. I'm sorry. I've taken up a lot of your time and haven't answered your question."

Greg cut in, "You've told us, Grandpa Roy. You've told us. We love each other and we love you also. Goodnight!"

MISTER, I AIN'T AFEERD UF NOBODY

The early morning mists hung heavily over McGlone Creek. Ghostly shapes took form along the hillside as the trees rose into and above the mists. Eric walked among the sweet scented honeysuckle, leading his brother's dog for their morning walk. He and his wife, Vera, had been visiting with his brother for a month now and each morning about six o'clock, he and Brandy would take a walk down the narrow dirt road leading away from the old farmhouse.

Early tomorrow morning, he and Vera would take his brother's wagon and two horses and ride to the train station in nearby Olive Hill. Eric was the principal of a small school in Ohio and now it was time for him to return home to get ready for the start of school. He would leave the wagon and horses with his sister and then board the train for Cincinnati.

Somewhere coming out of the quietness of the morning, there was a strange sound and Brandy seemed to want to move toward the creek bank. Moving carefully, they walked toward the sound, making sure there was no injured animal that might try to attack Brandy. It was almost impossible to see along the bank but as they moved toward the sound, Eric could tell it was not an animal but a human.

Hurrying now, he almost stumbled over the body of a small girl lying there on the side of the bank.

"What in the world are you doing here? And who are you?"

Eric bent down to see her better and saw she was having trouble with her right leg.

"This may be broken. Be very careful not to move until I can get a better look at it. Don't be afraid."

"Mister, I ain't afeered uf nobody."

"Well now, I'm glad to hear that."

After looking closer at her leg, he said, "I think you only have a bad sprain. I'm going to straighten the leg out. It may hurt quite a bit but we need to see how badly you are hurt."

"Owww! That hurts a mite, Mister. Doncha be so rough."

"I'm trying to be careful but it has to hurt some to get you moved. Who are you and what are you doing here?"

"I shore ain't agoin' ta talk with you, Mister. You might jest take me back ta Pap and I ain't agoin' back."

"Then I think you had best come up to the house with me and we can have a good breakfast and you can talk with the womenfolk. I can carry you or you can hold onto my arm, whichever you want."

"I'll go with ya but I ain't agoin' ta talk with them women neither. I'll have something ta eat, for which I thank ya, and then I'll just be on my way. Did ya see my horse? And I can walk by myself, thank you."

"You certainly are a sassy little girl for someone I found here in the valley who doesn't belong here. I never saw you around here before. But that's all right. If you don't want to talk with us, we'll just have to take you to town with us tomorrow and turn you over to the sheriff."

"You can't do that, Mister! He would take me home and I can't stand it there no more. I'll tell ya about it when we get ta the house. But doncha tell anyone else. Promise me that, Mister."

"We'll see."

She limped along behind Eric as he hurried toward the house.

"Here we are. Let's get you inside and fill up that stomach. Vera! Vera! We have a visitor for breakfast. I think you had best hurry out here."

With a dishtowel thrown over her shoulder, Vera hurried to the porch.

"My goodness! Where did you find her? Honey, who are you? I don't rightly remember seeing you around here. Do you live in the valley?"

"Well, ma'am. I don't want ta talk ta nobody, but yore man here, said he was going ta turn me over ta the sheriff if I didn't talk, so I'll tell ya my story. Yore man promised he wouldn't tell nobody and you have ta promise me too."

Vera bent over the little girl and wiped away some tears. "Honey, you tell me your story and we'll do whatever is best for you."

Eric's brother, Clarence, was out in the barn milking, and Lucy, Clarence's wife was in the henhouse gathering eggs to fix for breakfast. They would have to know the girl was here, but Eric wouldn't tell anyone else. He probably wouldn't see anyone before he left anyway.

Eric was twenty-six years old and Vera was twenty-four. They had been married for four years and had no children. The doctor had told them that it was not possible for them to have children, so Vera seemed to feel very close to this little girl who said she was twelve years old. She took the girl by the arm and guided her to the kitchen where there was a pan of hot water on the stove. Vera then fixed a pan so the girl could wash her hands and face. As the little one was washing, Lucy came in, heard the story, helped Vera finish the breakfast and began setting it on the table.

"Come on over here and sit by me. And don't you think we should know your name? My name is Vera and my husband is Eric. This nice lady is Lucy and her husband is Clarence. They live here and we all would like to help you. Why don't you sit here and fill up your plate and while you're eating, you can tell us about yourself. Maybe we can help you."

The little girl looked first at Vera, then at Eric. "Are you sure, Mister, that you'll take me ta the sheriff if I don't talk?"

"You can bet on that, little girl. But I'll keep my promise to you that I won't tell anyone about you if you'll tell us who you are and what you're doing here."

"Well, I don't know…"

She took up another biscuit, covered it with gravy and mixed an egg all up in it. "This shore is good, Ma'am. I ain't eaten like this since my ma died last year."

"I'm sorry about your mother, honey, but go on, tell us your story. We won't tell anyone."

"Well, my ma died a year ago and that left just my pap and me. He wuz 'awright fer awhile but then he took ta drinkin' and goin' out with some other wimmen and he jest seemed ta ferget about me. I had ta do the cookin' and all the housework. A few days ago, I don't recall how many—I'm all mixed up on the days—he cum home real drunk and when I didn't have nuthin' out fer him to drink, he slapped me across the face and knocked me against the wall. As I fell, my flour sack dress cum off me and he looked at me kinda funny, got up out of his chair, and cum toward me. I picked up my dress and put it around me but he tore it away, and picked me up in his arms and took me over ta the bed. This warn't the first time he had done that but he hadn't been drunk before, and he only held me up against him. I cried fer him ta quit, ta put me down, but he jest laughed and slobbered all over me."

She looked at Eric, and then turned her head away.

"Mister, I can't talk with ya and that other man, here in the room."

Eric got up, moved out on the porch and sat there in the swing watching the sun come up over the hills and slowly begin to burn the fog away.

In the kitchen, the little girl, who had told them her name was Delores, wiped away her tears and said to Vera, "Ma'am, I can't go on with this story. It's too hard ta talk about it."

"Delores, you do as you wish but it would be better if you could talk about it and then you could start forgetting about it. Do what you want to do."

Clarence had finished his breakfast and Lucy shooed him out to the porch with Eric.

"What's going on in there, Eric? Who is that little girl?"

"I don't know. The women are trying to get her to talk. I found her this morning down by the creek. Said she had been thrown off her horse. At first, I thought her leg was broken but I'm certain now that it's only a sprain. She has more fear than pain. We'll have to wait and see what the women say about her. She says she is twelve years old but I wonder if she isn't a bit older. Looks it to me."

Delores sat at the table a long time, took several long drinks of milk, looked up at Vera and said maybe she would tell about it.

"Pap laid me down on the bed and ya know, he tried ta do it to me."

With this, she broke into deep sobs and Vera put her arms around her and said maybe it would be best to talk about it another time.

"No, I'll go on. Pap wuz so drunk he couldn't get his pants down and as he wuz tryin', I got away. I run ta the barn and got my horse and rode away as fast as I could. I didn't have a saddle or nuthin' so I held on ta Maisey's mane. I 'spect we rode fer an hour or more before we stopped to rest. I dropped off ta sleep fer a little while and when I woke, I wuz afeered and got on Maisey and rode some more, maybe four hours, maybe a day, I don't know. We got lost in the fog, and some animal spooked Maisey and I fell off there where yore man found me. I guess Maisey run off. I never saw her again. That's about it, ma'am. I ain't agoin' back. It ain't right fer Pap to do that ta me. And that's a fact."

"Delores, that's quite a story. I wish you would let me tell Eric the rest of what you told me and then we can decide what to do with you. I don't even know your last name."

Lucy had been holding a hot towel on Delores's leg and kept muttering, "Poor little girl. What's going to happen to you?"

"I don't think I'll tell ya that, ma'am. Why don't ya take me along with ya when ya leave tomorrow? I won't be no trouble and when we get somewhere else, I'll leave and go my own way."

Vera and Lucy both started crying and Eric heard them and came into the room. Clarence had gone off to the barn to let the cows out into the pasture.

"What's happening in here? Is everything all right?"

Vera hugged him and said everything was fine.

"Delores, why don't you let me put you to bed and you can get some sleep? You'll be safe here with us. When you wake up, we three can have a long talk about what to do."

Lucy took Delores by the arm and led her to the bedroom and tucked her under some warm quilts. Almost immediately, she was asleep.

Vera and Eric talked a long time about Delores and what they should do.

"I can't let her go back to her Pap, as she calls him. And, if we turn her over to the sheriff, that's what will happen to her."

Almost in a whisper, Vera spoke, "Let's take her with us when we go home."

"Vera!" Eric almost shouted. "Do you know what you're saying? First of all, we have no right to do that, and secondly, we need to turn her over to the sheriff. I don't believe he will give her back to the father when he hears the story. And besides, to take her with us would be kidnapping and you know what that means. She can't live too far from here and I'm sure someone will know who she is. You can't do it, Vera. You just can't do it."

"Now calm down, Eric. I know all that. If we don't tell anyone, who will know about it? And you know as well as I do, the sheriff will not bother to help her. We don't know where she's from anyway. She may or may not be from this County. Let's take her with us and try to help her. We could tell everyone she's our little niece."

Lucy said she felt the sheriff would do nothing but take the little girl back to her pap. "Our sheriff here is not about to do anything to help anyone unless it helps him." Having overheard the conversation about taking the girl home, Lucy asked Vera, "How could a twelve year old be your niece when you have no brothers or sisters? I guess she could be Eric's niece. But I think the idea is preposterous."

"Yes, she could be your daughter. No one will know the difference when we get home anyway."

Eric nodded in agreement, looked at the longing in Vera's eyes, coughed, and said, "All right! Let's do it!"

Lucy, shocked at such an idea, "But Eric, that's kidnapping and going across the State line. What happens if someone comes looking for her? You best rethink your suggestion."

"I'm going to let Vera take a chance. And Delores seems to be agreeable. Just don't say anything to anyone and we'll keep quiet about it. If someday she wants to come back, well then, we'll let her."

Next morning, they packed their suitcases in the wagon; Eric went to the barn to get the horses and to tell Clarence they were leaving. Goodbyes were said and Vera wrapped Delores in some blankets, got out of the wagon, hugged Clarence and Lucy, and waved goodbye.

"We won't mention Delores to anyone. But if we hear anything about her, we will let you know."

Lucy called out as they drove away.

Eric was to leave the wagon at their sister's house and he was to leave her some fresh produce from the farm.

"Take care and have a good year at school."

They arrived at the train depot about an hour before the train was due to arrive. A wheel on the wagon had come loose and they were delayed.

"There won't be much time to visit with sis, Vera. You stay here with Delores and I'll take the wagon and horses up to her and will be right back. Why don't you sit here on the bench with the suitcases and best you don't talk to anyone unless it's the stationmaster? I doubt if he knows who we are so he won't question Delores being with us."

After coming back from his sister's, Eric purchased the tickets, handed them to the conductor and they settled in for the short ride to Cincinnati.

Delores cuddled up in Vera's arms and soon dropped off to sleep. She had never seen a train and was a little scared when it rolled into the station, but soon got used to the noise and smoke.

On the way, Eric and Vera talked about what to say to the people at home. They stuck with the niece story.

"Those schools down there in the mountains just aren't good enough. Too much tomfoolery, especially at the Superintendent's office and we want her to get a good education. I think we'll keep her with us until she finishes school. My sister-in-law is not well and really isn't able to care for her daughter at this time."

Vera explained the girl away to the neighbors and their friends.

Two years passed. Eric accepted a school position in another small town in Southern Ohio where the people readily accepted Delores as their niece. Nothing was ever said by them or to them, about her.

Time passed and Delores grew into a beautiful young girl. She attended the local high school where her grades were exceptionally good, graduating as top student in her class. She had dated a few boys but her interest was in her schoolwork and she was presented with a scholarship to a college in the East. When Eric and Vera went back to visit with Clarence and Lucy, they had arranged for a neighbor lady to care for Delores, not wanting to take a chance on her being recognized by anyone back on the Creek.

"I'm eighteen now, Mom."

She had started calling Eric and Vera dad and mom when they moved to the new town. Evidently no one thought anything about her calling them that instead of aunt and uncle, at least no one ever mentioned it.

"It's time for me to go on to college and be on my own. I've learned to love you both as my real mom and dad but I have to go on with my life. I'll be home to visit but I really have an urge to be on my own. Do you understand?"

"Of course we understand, dear. Come on home as much as you can and bring your friends if you want. We love you as if you were our own daughter and we want you to be happy whatever you may do."

Delores left that September for school. She often wrote letters and came home as much as she could. Nothing was ever said about her past and Clarence always mentioned to Eric that nothing was ever said about a missing girl.

After her second year, she wrote home that she was to going to Washington D.C. to work for the summer but she would be home before school started in the fall. But something happened that summer! Her letters became more infrequent and she didn't try to get home before school started. They heard from her in early winter and she said she would be home for Christmas and she had a surprise for them. She sounded the same as ever and Eric and Vera were excited as the time for her to arrive drew near.

Christmas came and went. New Year's came and still no word of Delores. There was a new contraption called a telephone installed in their house so Eric called the college and asked about her. He told the operator what he wanted and after waiting for some time, the operator came back on the phone and told him he would have to talk with the President of the college.

"Hello. This is President Burton speaking. How may I help you?"

Eric explained to the lady what they were trying to find out and said they were quite anxious to know about Delores.

"Sir. I don't know how to tell you this except to be quite honest with you. Your niece, Delores, told us here at school that she was going to go home to have her baby and she wouldn't be back to school. She left school about two weeks before Christmas. We assumed she was home with you since we never heard from her again. Maybe you should call the police. She isn't here and we haven't heard from her. We'll certainly cooperate in any way we can."

Eric hung up the phone. He was numb. He said nothing as he turned to Vera. Looking at him, she realized something was wrong.

"What is it, dear? What's the matter?"

"It's over. Our life means nothing now. Whatever did we do to cause her to do what she did?"

"Caused who to do what?"

Eric sat on the sofa and told Vera what President Burton had told him. They both cried.

"What are we going to do, Eric? We can't just let this pass by as if nothing happened. What about the baby? We have to do something."

"I'm going to visit President Burton. Maybe some of Delores's classmates can give us some information. I don't want to go to the police yet. I'm leaving on the next train."

The following morning at four o'clock, Eric was on the train headed for the school.

"Come in, Sir. I've called Pam, Delores's roommate and she has something to say which may help you. You may use my office to speak with her as long as you want."

She left the room and Pam stood there with Eric not knowing what to say.

"Pam, can you tell us anything? Delores was our life. We're lost without her."

"No, Sir."

Pam was nervous but she was willing to talk.

"All I know is she left school because she wanted to go home to have her baby. She said she was going to surprise you at Christmas and was excited because she knew how happy you would be about it. But you know, for some reason, I didn't believe her. I felt she was making up the story of how happy you would be. When she was alone, she would cry a lot and often I would come into the room and she would be wiping away tears. I don't know. Things didn't seem right. I wish I could tell you more because we all loved her and the entire school is worried about her.

"Thank you, Pam. I'll go back home and see what we can find out. I'll have to report her as missing and see what the authorities can do. Do you think there was anyone who would harm her? I'm sure the police will want to talk with you and others but I'd like to know first."

"That's all I know. I'll be happy to talk with the authorities if I can help. Please let me know what you find out."

"Thank you again."

Eric left the office and walked slowly back to the train station where he caught the next train for home. He wasn't sure what to tell the police but after he and Vera discussed her disappearance, the authorities were notified but all searches proved fruitless. Eric had written Clarence to see if perhaps she had gone back there. He still hadn't told anyone about her past and didn't intend to if he could help it.

When one of the officers came to tell Eric they couldn't locate her but would keep trying, he and Vera wept bitterly.

"How can a person just disappear? There must be somewhere else you can look or something you can do."

"We will keep on trying, Sir. We have sent her picture to other police departments so someone will locate her eventually. It may take time. But I'm sure she will show up."

"Thank you." Eric saw the officer to the door, turned to Vera and they held each other for a long time.

*****

Many years passed. Nothing at all had been found about the disappearance of Delores. Clarence and Lucy had passed away and Eric had retired and he and Vera returned to the Creek where they built a beautiful home on the old family property. Time had helped take away some of the memories, but buried deep within their souls, the memory of Delores lingered. Eric thought about her each time he passed the spot where he had found her on the fog covered morning many years ago. He had forgotten how many years but since he was now seventy, and he had been twenty-six at the time, he figured it to be over forty. They had checked from time to time with various police departments but there was no trace and now they accepted the fact that she was probably dead.

Eric now had a dog of his own and each morning, he and Casey would take a walk down around the creek and sometimes they would wander off into the hills.

It was a late April morning when Eric left the house to take his daily walk. It was hot but the redbud and dogwood were at their peak and Eric liked to walk back along the hills to see the trees and was carrying some branches of dogwood back home where Vera would make a bouquet. As he neared the house, he saw Vera in her flower garden watering her rose bushes. He waved to her and joined her on the porch swing where they enjoyed some cold lemonade. As they spoke of the beauty of the morning and talked about what they were going to do that day, an automobile appeared in their driveway.

A beautiful lady got out of the car as Vera walked to the porch steps to meet her.

"Good morning. Come up on the porch and get out of the sun. This is going to be a hot day. My name is Vera and this is my husband, Eric. May we help you in some way?"

With a lovely smile, the young lady reached for Vera's hand.

"You know, Vera, I think with your permission, I would rather call you grandma."

"Why would you call me that, dear? I think it's a beautiful thing to do but I don't believe we know you, or if we do, we've forgotten about you."

Eric walked over from the swing. "Wait a minute! What did you say you wanted to call her?"

Again smiling, the young lady said to him. "I said I would like to call her grandma and I would like to call you grandpa."

Eric and Vera looked at each other and wondered who this woman might be. They didn't recognize her but figured she must be someone who had left here several years ago. But she wasn't old enough to have been in the valley when Clarence lived here.

They offered the lady a seat in a rocking chair and as she sat down she said to Eric, "Mister, I ain't afeered uf no body!"

Suddenly Eric caught on. "I've only heard that from one woman and you sure aren't her. Who are you?" He held on to Vera's hand and had a hard time to keep from shaking.

"I understand your shock. Getting up from her chair, the lady held Vera in her arms. I'm Delores's daughter and she told me you were the only grandparents I ever had. I've been trying to find you for several months now. Let's sit down and I'll tell you my story."

Pausing… "That is, if you want to hear my story?"

Flabbergasted, both Eric and Vera choked up and couldn't say anything. The young woman again put her arms around Vera and hugged her tightly and did the same thing to Eric.

"Please let me tell you my story and then I'll leave and won't bother you if that's what you prefer. I didn't know whether to look you up or not, but finally decided it was time I had some relatives to visit."

"Oh my! Oh dear! Yes! Yes! Please sit down. We are so shocked. But here, have a glass of lemonade and tell us all about yourself. Eric, can you believe this is happening? Oh my! I'm so nervous."

"Mother named me after you. My name is also Vera. Susan Vera, but I go by the name of Susan. I don't know what to say or where to begin. I had planned to come and see you, spend a few hours, tell you my story as mother made me promise to do, and then leave. This is a beautiful spot. Already I have a feeling of being home, not just home in a house. I have that, but home in spirit, home with my loved ones, and I don't have that."

Vera spoke out between sobs. "Where is your mother? How very much we've missed her and we want so desperately to see her. So many years have passed. Oh my, Eric, I can't settle down!"

"Mother passed away many years ago but before she did, she wrote me a long letter and on the outside she wrote that I was not to open it until my thirtieth birthday. That was a mystery to me but I did as she wished, although there were many times I reached for it to open it. About two years ago, on my thirtieth birthday, I opened the letter. I was out of the country but had taken the letter with me because I knew I would be gone on my birthday. Mother and I had talked many times after I got old enough to understand what she was saying. She told me her entire story, leaving out nothing except who you were. She told me I would find that out another day. She hurt deeply inside as she talked to me and I sensed she missed you very much but couldn't make herself get in touch with you. I told her I thought she was hurting you more by staying away than by telling me her story."

"What could have possibly hurt us more than her staying away?"

Eric, too, was nervous now and at the same time he felt like it was a homecoming for his family.

"You, of course, know about mother's first two years of school. When mother told you she would be home for Christmas and didn't show up, she had found out she was pregnant. Remember she said she had a surprise for you? That was the surprise. She wanted so much to let you know and to hold on to your love. She really needed you. But then, she started thinking how disappointed you would have been with her and how hurt you would have been, so she decided never to come back.

Mother had been out with one of the boys from town, and on their way back to her dormitory, she had been raped by him and became pregnant. She reported it to the police in town but they laughed at her and said she had probably brought it on herself. You see, it so happened that the boy was the son of the Chief of Police. Realizing that nothing was going to be done, mother left the school, telling them she was going home and would not return to school. She obtained a job in Washington D.C. working for the Federal Government and after I was born, she started traveling, taking me with her whenever possible. Her job was in public relations for the Senate and she had to be away from home quite often. We were very close as I grew up and when I was about seventeen, we took a vacation together in Cape Cod and mother told me everything about her life. She told me how her 'pap' had almost raped her when she was just a young girl, how she had run away and had been found by you, and then when she went away to school, what had happened to her. She felt that men had abused her twice in her life and you might not understand. She never married and never had much to do with men after that. She did try to contact the boy who was my father but he had been killed in a motorcycle wreck soon after the rape episode. He was a heavy drinker and his family denied that he could possibly be the father. So, it was just the two of us.

One day, she came home in a hurry and said she had an opportunity to go to Europe and I could go if I wanted to. She would be there about a month and it would not cost us anything to go. There was to be a conference in Paris and she had to attend but she would be with me every evening and on weekends and we could visit all the wonderful places in Paris. I was 'growing' up and chose not to go, so mother, I think a bit disappointed with me, made arrangements for me to stay with a friend while she was gone. She was to go to New York to catch the ship to Paris and had just a few days to get ready. The next day on her way to work, mother was hit by a car and was killed instantly. It took me years to overcome this grief. I also began working for the government, but perhaps I should have gone somewhere else. It seemed that everyday something happened which reminded me of her. She had given me the letter with written instructions for me not to open it; when I did open it, I found out who you were and where you last lived. I went to the town in Ohio but you had been long gone and no one there knew where you were. I went back to Washington and had some friends start to trace you down. Finally, a gentleman friend of my husband told us he had found someone with your name here in Kentucky. I took it from there and here I am."

Sitting still for a long time, the three of them listened to the birds singing, smelled the aroma of the flowers, and just seemed to be lost in thought.

To no one in particular, Susan spoke up. "I was planning to leave right away but if you'll have me, I'd like to stay a little longer. I'll have to leave soon but I want to visit with you some more. I'd like to see the place where mother grew up. Grandfather, show me where you found her. She told me what happened. Did you ever find the horse? Did anyone ever come looking for her?"

"No, Susan. We never found the horse. We didn't even bother to look for it. We had to leave right away so there was not time to look for the horse and my brother said no one ever came looking for her. She was a lovely young girl. We missed her so much."

They spent the rest of the day getting better acquainted and looking around the farm.

Next morning, Eric took Susan with him and they went down to the creek to the spot where her mother had been thrown from her horse. It was by an old wagon trail and was no longer in use since the automobile had become popular. There were a lot of ferns growing around the area and moss had covered much of the bank of the creek.

Susan took off her shoes and waded in the water stepping carefully so she wouldn't step on a sharp stone. She then joined Eric on the bank and they talked about her mother, how she had been treated, and both wondered why she hadn't come back.

"You know we lived in Ohio. We left here the next day so there was nothing here for her but we tried our best to give her a good home. We both loved her."

Eric let his thoughts roam back to the day he found her and the good times he and Vera had had with her.

"I know you loved her and she loved you both. For some reason she couldn't face you after she had been raped. She thought you might think she was that kind of woman. A woman to lead men on. Mother felt she had wronged you but didn't know how to make it up to you."

Susan stayed four days there on McGlone Creek with Eric and Vera and then she had to go back to her home. "I have a wonderful husband and he is very understanding when I have to be away."

Eric packed Susan's bag in her car and walked around to say goodbye. They all hugged and had a good cry.

"You're welcome here anytime, Susan. Next time, bring your husband and plan to stay awhile."

Eric hugged her once more, opened her door, and then he walked away so Vera could talk with her.

"Goodbye, dear. Please come back to see us and come soon."

Closing the car door, Susan waved goodbye and drove down the driveway to the road, disappearing in a cloud of dust.

*****

Exactly three months from the day she left them, they received a telephone call from Susan's husband.

"Susan didn't want you to know but she had cancer and died this morning. She had written a little note for you and asked me to tell you what it said. I don't understand it, but it says, "Mister, I ain't afeered uf no body!""

SPIRITS OF THE CREEK

He sat there in the enveloping darkness like a sentinel guarding the valley. The old man, Sammy, had been watching his three 'coon dogs play in the field off to the side of the hill from where he sat. He lit up his pipe, leaned back against the beech tree and watched down below, where the darkness had become almost complete. Here on the hill, the shadows were creeping ever closer to the top, and the stars in the heavens, were beginning to twinkle brightly. It was going to be a hot, clammy night and he had told Janice, his wife, he was going up on the ridge to see if the dogs could find some 'coons to chase.

"Remember Sammy, tomorrow is Homecoming Day and we have to get the food ready and go to church in the morning."

"I know, Janice. I won't be out late. I just want to get a breath of fresh air and there doesn't seem to be any coolness down here right now. I'll take 'ol Blue and Red with me, and Sadie if she wants to go. We won't be long."

Janice knew that Sammy, her husband of almost forty-five years, liked to be outside on the hot nights and there wasn't much he liked to do better than to take the hounds out for a 'coon hunt. He would likely be out most of the night and she would have a hard time getting him ready to go tomorrow. Their boys would come over to the house and take care of the milking in the morning and she would go gather the eggs for breakfast.

Tomorrow was to be celebrated as the one-hundredth homecoming on the Creek and a large crowd was expected. Some said it would be more than one hundred years but it was not known for sure since no one had kept any records. It didn't make any difference to Janice. She enjoyed visiting with her old friends and the day was something she always looked forward to. The homecoming was always held the second Sunday in August and normally there would be from one hundred to two hundred people there. Tomorrow, there would be more than that, at least the folks in the valley hoped so.

Sammy sat there on the top of the ridge surveying the little valley where his ancestors had settled almost two hundred years ago. The engraved tombstone of old Owen showed he was born in the year of seventeen seventy-seven, and old courthouse records showed he was in this valley about the year eighteen hundred with his family. His gravesite was just down the road from where Sammy sat. The family cemetery was on up the valley across from the old school/church house near the area where the homecoming was held.

As Sammy thought about the valley in the old days, he muttered to himself. "Kind of funny. None of us ever knew where Owen had his home. Must have been down near his grave. I expect it was a log cabin of some sort. I'll have to ask Melvina if she knows. I hope she can be here tomorrow."

Complete darkness was now upon him. As he reached to light his lantern he heard Sadie and Red begin to give out their call telling they had found the tracks of a 'coon. Shortly he would hear the baying of 'Ol Blue telling they had treed it. He could recognize the sound of each dog and Sammy knew when he or she had treed something. When that happened, he would follow the sound and find the 'coon. Sammy wouldn't kill the creature because none of the family liked 'coon meat and it would be a senseless killing, something Sammy didn't like to do. He never liked to kill any of the wild animals, and always talked to his three boys about how wrong he thought it was.

Sammy stood up, tapped out his pipe, stretched, and as he did, the headlights of a car penetrated the darkness down below. It was moving slowly, following the narrow dirt road that wound along the creek bank. Obviously the car was headed up the valley and Sammy wondered who it might be at this hour. Not many people traveled this road at night and when someone did, it was usually some family member. He thought about it for a bit, then turned up his lantern to get more light and moved off toward the sound of the dogs. He watched the tail lights of the car disappear around the bend and then forgot about it.

*****

David was searching for the entrance to the valley where his family had lived in their early years. It had been maybe twenty years since he had been here and he was trying to find the road, following his sister's directions. He was getting interested in genealogy and thought this valley would be a good place to do some research since a "pocket" of the family had settled here many years ago.

"I wish I hadn't been held up so long at the store. Now it's going to be dark and it will be harder to find the road," David thought.

He had stopped to buy some supplies at a nearby local grocery and since it was late Saturday afternoon , the people were out doing their shopping. The grocer had been busy and David had to wait his turn. He was used to the big city markets where you did your own shopping. But here, the grocer took what you needed off his shelves as you asked for it. Then, to make the trip 'complete,' he had a flat tire and had to change it in the fading light of the day.

"I believe this is it." Muttering to himself, he turned up the now dark valley and began to slowly follow the little dirt road. His sister, Rosalie, had told him of the winding road and she also said she had heard there had been several deer killed because of cars running into them.

After he had driven perhaps a mile up the valley, he thought he saw a light coming from the top of a nearby hill. This was the first sign of people he had seen although he had passed a few houses with no lights burning.

"Funny," he mused. "That light seems to be rather tiny and it's moving. Maybe someone lives up there and they're going to the outhouse with a lantern to guide them. I can't see much out here anyway."

Driving on, he soon reached the white church building he was looking for and pulled into the parking area beside it and parked his van. As he got out of the vehicle, he was in total darkness. He vaguely remembered the building, which was once a one-room schoolhouse but Rosalie said now it was used mostly as a church.

Looking up into the night sky, he thought, "My goodness, look at those stars. I don't ever remember seeing as many stars as there are up there now. They look like tiny lights shining through some sort of shield."

Taking his flashlight, he shined the beam around him and picked out the church house on the other side of the lot. There were two outhouses, one on each side of the building but nothing more. The creek ran along the edge of the parking area but he couldn't see it because of the brush growing beside its banks.

David had decided to come to the Creek and spend the night out in the open so he could get a feel of how the old man, his Great, Great, Grandfather Owen, must have felt when he first arrived here with his family. "I expect this is pretty much the same as it was when Owen arrived here in the valley," he muttered to himself.

His thoughts were roaming as he prepared to settle down for the night. "There's a road now and a few houses, and I imagine most of this was timber land when he arrived. Wonder what made him choose this valley to settle in?" David was curious and planned to do some looking around after the homecoming tomorrow. He hoped to meet some of the old timers to see what information they could give him about the settling of the valley.

Spreading his sleeping bag in the back of his van, David settled down to sleep. He wanted to be up very early in the morning before anyone came around. He remembered seeing the mists rising up in the hills when he was here with his father many years ago. Chidingly, his dad had told him the mists were clouds going back up into the sky to spend the day. David had a lot of memories as he thought back to the days, those many years ago, when he would come here with his father. He remembered the roosters crowing, the cows calling out to the farmer to come and milk them. Now, he could hear the frogs singing out over by the creek, the whippoorwills calling from the woods around him. The crickets, or whatever, were loud tonight. And……the mosquitoes made their presence felt.

Thinking to himself as he lay there, "This is not a bad life, I guess. I suppose it's difficult to make a living here but it's certainly a lovely place to visit. That honeysuckle smells real good."

David, a tall, well built, red headed young man, looked like his father's side of the family, or so everyone told him. He hadn't thought much about it until he started tracing his lineage and met, through books and mail, others of his family. He had become interested in this hobby and had spent many hours in libraries and courthouses throughout the country and some days in Ireland. Relaxing and remembering all these things, he soon dropped off into a deep sleep.

*****

A fluttering of the night wind! An eerie sound! Leaves of the trees moving in odd ways! Night owls calling out their hoots in strange sounds! Bats were flying in wild patterns! What was going on all up and down the Creek?

*****

Old Sammy, out on the hill 'coon hunting with his dogs, suddenly felt the strange sensations; the dogs who were just a moment ago, baying at a treed 'coon, suddenly became quiet; a young man who was asleep in the churchyard in his van, was wakened by unseen noises. A woman at home waiting for her man to come back from hunting; felt strange powers within her home. Her kerosene lamps were turned up and she wondered what caused the strange feelings!

*****

All over the valley and up in the hills, the Spirits of the Creek were gathering for this Homecoming Day. Those who had long ago departed and those who were newcomers to the eternal life, were all coming together to celebrate this one hundredth celebration. They had been released from their celestial duties to attend this big day in the valley. And even though they couldn't be seen by human eyes, they would be there to visit with each other and to recall happy days they had spent here. Their presence among the humans would cause some unwanted sensations, but they would try and be very careful not to cause any undue disturbances. Before they had been released from their duties, they had been instructed not to cause any problems among the gathered people. "You are there to visit with your fellow spirits and not to be any problem to the humans gathered. Do not by any means, scare or disturb anyone!" The spirit world also has "spirits in charge" and the special instructions were given to all.

Many of the spirits had gathered upon the hill, strangely enough, near where the old 'coon hunter was moving to find his dogs. This is why Sammy had felt the strange sensations come over him. Some of the spirits had gone to visit the old home place and this is why the woman, Janice, had felt as she did. And some had gone to the church/school building to visit and this is why

David thought he had heard noises. A few others had gone to roam the hills as they had when they were in human form and the dogs had sensed their presence.

*****

"Do you suppose he'll come?"

"I don't know. If he does, I hope he brings his wife, Polly. I haven't heard about her lately. She was a hard working woman."

The spirits were talking about old man Owen and his family. Many of them, in fact, most of them, were direct decedents of Owen, and they all wanted to visit with him again. They liked to hear the stories of how he settled this valley, what it was like, and why he had stayed. He was for certain the patriarch and they all looked forward to seeing him.

"You know, there has been a lot of speculation lately as to where Owen settled when he first came here. That boy, David, up at the church house, is trying to tie the family together but he is getting some of his information wrong and just tonight, I heard Sammy thinking to himself where Owen had settled."

The spirits continued to gossip among themselves.

"I know. But there's no way he can find correct records. Most of us couldn't write and no one was interested anyway. We just didn't keep any records."

"I suppose so. However, it would be interesting to be able to tell him of the founding of McGlone Creek. There is no way he will ever know the true story."

Several other spirits chimed in. "Isn't there any way we can get the message to David? He seems like a fine young man and is trying hard to get us all sorted out in his mind. We'd sure like for him to know."

"Now you know what our instructions are. And there is no way we can communicate with them anyway. All of those people who think they can communicate with us are real phonies. You all know we can't do it. Someday when he joins us, he'll learn and we'll all sit around and laugh with him."

The spirit who had been placed in charge had joined the others. He had lived with his family in the old family home and his untimely death had caused much sorrow in the valley.

The spirits of those who had passed on and had gathered to celebrate the homecoming were moving on the winds all over the valley remembering days spent on Earth and visiting with others who had also lived there.

Eager to be a part of the celebration, one spirit, who had been a twin back on Earth, was creating quite a stir among the others. It had been trying to communicate with the humans and of course, had no way to do so. The leader had to take him aside and speak rather harshly to him about disobeying him.

*****

On the day of Homecoming, several people gathered around David as he talked about what he had found concerning the family name in his research. Sammy, who now lived in the old family home, was standing there, and overheard David speak about staying in his van last night trying to get a feel of the area when Owen had settled in the valley.

"David, you aren't the fellow who drove up the road last night after dark, are you?"

"Yes sir, I am. I didn't know anyone saw me. There were no lights on in any of the houses. I did think I saw a light up on a hill, but it was a tiny glow and didn't last long."

"Well, that was me. I was out 'coon hunting and saw your headlights as I was sitting there waiting for the dogs to tree a 'coon. I wondered who that might be coming up the road so late."

David talked with some other folks and as the day drew to a close, people began to leave in their cars and some walked to their nearby homes. The many tables had been cleared of food and it had been a good day. About three hundred came to visit and to eat the wonderful food that was spread out on the tables.   Most of them had brought dishes to share with the others. After the meal was over, there was still plenty of food remaining.

After most of the folks had left, Sammy walked over to David. "David, why don't you come on over to the house for awhile. I have some family pictures I'd like for you to see and maybe we can see how we're related to the others."

David readily agreed.

As they walked down the little road to the house, Sammy began talking to David about the family and how he had heard from his parents about the 'old timers'.

"David, your grandfather and my father were first cousins. I'm sure about that. I have some pictures from the time your grandfather used to come visit us and bring your father when he was small. I don't remember your dad bringing you here though. As a matter of fact, your grandfather had a twin who died when he was just a young man, in his teens I think. Let's see now. There was my father, your grandfather, Aunt Rosie, and Finley who used to play together. Finley was the twin. Your grandfather left here to go up north and used to come back at least once a year. I remember he liked to come back and 'explore' the hills. My father told me that Aunt Rosie and your Grandfather Charles were always restless and wanted to go away from the farm. But when they got older, they had changed their minds and always wanted to come back, but there was nothing here to come back to."

Janice greeted Sammy at the door, said hello to David, and they sat down on the porch to watch the sun settle behind the hills. Some of the visitors to the valley were still leaving and as they passed the house, they waved and called goodbye.

"I'll fix something to eat if anyone wants anything." Janice got up from the swing, walked toward the front door, heading for the kitchen.

"Not me." David laughed and wondered how his stomach could possibly hold anything more. "I think maybe I had better go get my car before it gets too dark. You go ahead and eat if you wish."

"I don't want anything either." Sammy stood up, rubbed his stomach, walked out to the road to say goodbye to an old friend. "When you get back, David, park your car there by the house, and plan to stay the night. I'll get the pictures. It'll take some time to look at all of them and we can have a good visit as we look. We would sure like for you to stay."

"I'd like that. I don't want to be any bother to you, though."

David walked off up the road to get his car, stopped to talk with some folks just leaving, and marveled at the number of people who had come back to the valley just for this day.

That evening as they sat at the table looking at the old pictures, a feeling came over David that he was being watched. Sammy was there with him so he wasn't the one watching. Janice was in the kitchen cleaning up her dishes from the homecoming dinner. No one else was in the house. It was a strange feeling and he kept looking around.

There was an unearthly eeriness about the room. David couldn't explain how he felt but wondered if Sammy felt the same.

Just then, Sammy spoke up. "David, I have the strangest feeling. I feel we're being watched as we look at these pictures. A minute ago, I would have sworn this picture of Charles and Finley moved. We certainly have strange imaginations, haven't we?"

Just then, several of the pictures fell to the floor. It was as though a wind had blown them off the table. But there was no wind!

The two men looked at each other, wondering what was happening. When Sammy picked up the pictures, the picture of Finley was on top.

David, this is the picture you put back in the album a minute ago. How did it get on the floor?"

*****

The Spirits were hovering over the table. Suddenly, Finley waved his arms and several pictures fell off the table.

The Spirit who had been placed in charge for the day said, "I know you used to be Finley and you were always playing tricks on your brother when you were a human, but we can't do that any more and you are completely wrong when you try to let them know you are here. I used to live here also, although a long time before you did. I too, have memories of the good days, but we cannot do anything to these people."

"Come on, all of you. It's time we go. It's been a great day for all of us, and for me, it was certainly good to visit with you again. Next year, some of these people we saw today, will probably be with us so we can gather again to celebrate."

Now spirits cannot have tears, cannot show emotion, cannot have lonely feelings. Cannot be sad. Or so it says in the book!

With suddenness, all of the spirits left the house. Some would linger in the valley; some would go off to other homes and distant places to watch over their human counterparts.

Later, they met on the top of the hill where they had entered the valley. With gratitude in their hearts for being allowed to be back on the Creek, they slowly ascended up into the soft blown winds of the evening.

Early next day, David left. When he reached the crossroad leading away from the valley entrance, he stopped the car, walked over to the bridge crossing the creek, to take one more look up the valley. Suddenly, a sprinkle of rain fell on him and he looked up into the cloudless sky, wondering what had happened. Moving quickly across the blue sky was a tiny dark cloud.

David was certain he heard from somewhere above him, a sound of 'hee hee, hee hee!'

SUNRISE----------SUNSET

She had been getting up at five o'clock every morning as long as she could remember. Her mother once told her that when she was a baby, she always awoke at five o'clock. Now she was sixty-five years old, stooped over a bit, but full of her always present vim and vigor. Grandmother, whom they called Ma, was short, with long hair tied up in a bun on top of her head. She was always cheerful, even at the end of a long day that was normal for the country wife she was. Her routine was the same each day except on Sunday when she prepared herself for worship at the little white church house just up the road from the two-story farm home, whitewashed so that it shone in the sunshine. She called the house a beacon to guide the Lord.

Ma would come down the stairs, rinse her face and wash her hands in the wash pan sitting on the stove that kept the water warm. She then would go out to the henhouse to gather eggs for the day with a stop at the outhouse, and then back into the house to wash again, and begin to prepare breakfast for the family. She and pa had moved in with their son, Benny, to help him take care of his ailing wife, Annie. They also enjoyed three grandchildren, Johnny, Junior, and Betty Jane, now grown to adults. The two grandsons were helping their dad take care of the farm and pa would do what he could do although his arthritis kept him from doing what he wanted to do. He did what he could to help and when it came time to harvest tobacco, he was at his best. Said the smell of the tobacco leaves helped his bones!

This morning when ma came back into the house with the eggs in her apron, her granddaughter, Betty Jane, greeted her. Being up this early was different because Betty Jane was always the one to sleep in if she could get away with it.

"Good morning, sweetie! You're up early today."

With a slight hesitation in her voice and with a worried look on her face, she told ma she needed to talk with her and she thought early morning would be the best time.

"I'm glad you want to talk with me, Betty Jane. I think I know what you want to tell me but go ahead. I'll listen while I get breakfast started." Getting the flour out of the pantry, she started to mix in the milk and stirred the mixture until it was just right for flapjacks. She had started the fire in the wood burning cook stove and had greased the frying pans in which she would fry the 'jacks.

"I don't know how to tell you, Ma. I'm afraid!"

"Don't be, honey. I know what you want to tell me so go ahead and put it in your own words."

"You mean you know? How could you? I've never told anyone."

"Honey. I've had seven children. Don't you think I know what's wrong with a woman when she is sick every morning? Oh yes. I've heard you get up while I was down here in the kitchen. Not much you can do that your old Ma don't know about. Who is he? And how far along are you?"

Hesitating again, Betty replied, "Ma, I'm so sorry and upset. I didn't mean to do it but we got carried away and before we could stop, it had happened. It's Billy Bob Kryster. He said we would get married right away and I told him dad would be upset with him. He's afraid to come here until I tell all of you know. I think I'm about two months pregnant but I don't know how to tell for sure."

Ma put the flapjack dough in the skillet while they talked and she began to make the coffee as the household began to stir. One of the boys came in and was surprised to see Betty Jane. "My goodness! To what do we owe this early morning visit? I'll bet Billy Bob is coming courtin' today! Is that right, little sister?"

"Hush up, Johnny. You just hush up." Crying, she rushed from the room only to bump into her father, Benny, as he pulled up his suspenders and walked into the kitchen. "Well my goodness! Look at this, won't you. Our princess is up already and looks like she has been putting onions in the eggs. Or, is it something else?" Walking over to the stove, "I see we are being treated to flapjacks and syrup this beautiful day!"

Now Junior walked in and the five of them stood in the kitchen, knowing something was not right this morning. Benny said, "All right now, what is it? What's going on? Something is amiss in the family and I don't like it a bit. Where's pa? He isn't sick, is he?"

"No, he isn't!"

Ma told them to sit down while she finished making the flapjacks, and when they were browned properly, she put them on the table and made the family wait to eat until pa said his thanks to the Lord.

"Now all of you listen up. Betty Jane has something to tell you and I don't want any sass from any of you and that includes you, Benny. I'll handle this situation so just be calm, all of you."

"Yes, Ma!" Laughing at her, Benny got up and helped her to her seat and sat back down.

Betty Jane began to cry and great sobs came up from her throat.

"O Land o' Goshen, Betty Jane. You best learn to be a woman and right now is a good time to start. You tell them or I will." Ma looked at her, told her to wipe away her tears, and told the rest of them to get on with the eating before the food got cold.

In between her crying, Betty Jane told them about her and Billy Bob and how they were going to get married. Shocked was the word! Benny sat speechless. The two boys looked at baby sister and didn't know what to say but pa broke the ice when he said, "He's a good boy. Got some growing up to do but you could do worse, Betty Jane."

Benny got up, walked out to the porch, slamming the door as he went. Ma motioned for the rest of them to stay seated and she got up and went out to join Benny as he walked to the barn.

"What did I do wrong, Ma? Why would she do such a thing? And her mother is so sick. What will she think?"

"I don't know what she will think, Benny. Betty Jane made a mistake just as so many others have done through the years. She's truly sorry but she needs your support and understanding and more than that, she desperately needs your love right now. She's a precious darling but she is growing up and as I said, she made a mistake. I think you need to go back in there and talk to her alone. Then you both need to go tell Annie. I think she will be fine if she sees you support Betty Jane. Then I think you need to have Billy Bob come here and find out what his intentions are before rushing to any wrong decisions. There, you've heard what I think. Now you have to do what you need to do. Remember though, we all love Betty Jane and she needs us to show that love for her."

Walking back to the house and into the kitchen, silence greeted her. Betty Jane started to cry again and Junior said, "Come on sister, quit crying. I'll go take care of Billy Bob for you. I thought he was my friend and he did this thing to my sister."

"You'll do no such thing, Junior." Ma looked seven feet tall as she beat on the table with her spoon as they had all begun to talk at once. "Betty Jane made a mistake and it's a mistake any of you could make. Now don't go being so righteous with me. I know what goes on in the hayloft with you and those Haney girls. You think me and your pa were born yesterday?"

Pa spoke up. "Let's finish our breakfast and go to work. Your dad and Betty Jane need to talk, and Ma, best we stay out of this unless we are asked for advice." Mumbling to himself, he said, "Somebody around here needs advice and it sure ain't me!"

Benny had come back to the house as ma suggested. He looked at Betty Jane and she began to cry again. "Dad, I'm so sorry. I love you and mommy so much and I'm sorry I've hurt you. I'm going upstairs to tell mommy right now and then I'll get my things together and leave if you want. Billy Bob said we could go to Carter to get married if need be."

Benny stood there a long time looking at her. Finally he said, "Daughter, let's me and you go out on the porch and sit in the swing for awhile. We need to talk about some things. Boys, you go on now and begin the plowing. Junior you take the double tree out of the barn and hitch up the horses. I'll be along after while but you go on and get started. Johnny, you be careful of that old mule. She's been a mean one lately." Shooing them out, ma took pa by the arm and said they needed to walk out in the pasture to see how the new calves were doing.

Benny and Betty Jane sat on the porch for a long time and then they went upstairs to where Annie was and being very careful not to hurt her, Benny took her in his arms and carried her down to her seat on the porch. The sun was coming up above the hills and the day promised to be a good one. She asked what the occasion was that she got to come downstairs so early.

Holding Benny's hand, she squeezed it and told him he was such a good husband and she would soon be better and could help out with the house. Hugging Betty Jane, she told her she was a beautiful woman.

Both Benny and Betty Jane knew that Annie would never recover and her time with them was growing shorter. All the family was aware of it but no one ever let on that they knew.

Streaks of red lit up the morning sky and the roosters were crowing in the barnyard. A long moo came from several of the cows and Benny said he had to go soon to do the milking but he and Betty Jane wanted to talk with Annie first. Smiling at Betty, he said to Annie, "Maybe I'd better tell you the good news and then you can talk with Betty while I go and attend to the chores."

He then very carefully told her about Betty Jane getting married to Billy Bob and she had his blessing and hoped that Annie would see fit to give hers also. "That Billy Bob is a good boy, Annie. He will fit in nicely here on the farm and we can use his help what with Johnny going off on his own soon. I 'spect Junior will want to go also so we will need an extra hand here. Pa is not much help these days with his arthritis and such. What do you say? Shall we send Betty up to Billy Bob's house and have him come to supper tonight?"

"Oh yes. Let's do just that." Giving Betty Jane a big hug, she told her to go and ask Billy Bob for supper tonight and they could discuss the plans.

With tears flowing down her cheeks, Betty Jane looked at her dad and hugged him as he started to leave and whispered in his ear, "Dad, I love you. Thank you for handling this so well. You and mommy are wonderful."

"I'll hitch up the buggy for you and you get on with what you have to do. Just make sure Billy Bob is here tonight. We want to put all this behind us so you can get on with your lives as well as letting us enjoy your mommy's last few days with us. You know, don't you, that her time is short?"

Betty Jane nodded, ran back upon the porch, hugged her mother and left for Billy Bob's.

*****

Betty Jane was the youngest of three children of Benny and Annie McGlone. She was now a young lady of nineteen and was a pretty girl with deep brown long hair and azure eyes to compliment her just the right size smile.

From her early years she had always been a tomboy, keeping up with Junior and Johnny, her older brothers, in most everything they did. She and a playmate, Billy Bob, gave absolute fits to the

125

brothers. When Junior and Johnny got tired of them being around, they would escape to their private place, where Billy Bob would tell her stories of wild animals and big cities and things which would make her heart throb with anxiety.

"How do you know these things, Billy Bob? You've never even been off the Creek."

"My dad told me all about them. He said there are animals that are bigger than any horses and some fish are bigger than ships. He's been to big cities where buildings are bigger than our hills!"

Billy Bob's dad had come to this country when he was a small boy and he would sit by the fire on winter nights and tell about the 'old country' and how his family had come here on a small ship. Billy Bob would listen to these stories and tell them to Betty Jane and they would giggle and pretend they were sailors and cooks on the ships.

Billy Bob had been nine and Betty Jane was seven when they were roaming the hills back up the ridge from where Billy Bob lived. They discovered a small hole in a limestone cliff and when they crawled into the hole, they found a large opening inside, somewhat like a cave, and pretending to hide from pirates, they both agreed they would always meet here, and they called it their 'secret place.'

As they grew up, they continued coming to the cave to talk, and eventually grew out of the age of imagination. They would talk about what they wanted to be and where they would live when they got older, and both made a vow to be best friends forever.

As the years passed and no one else found their secret place, young children-playmates soon became young man-and–woman, and temptations began to creep in. They would smoke corn silk together, and once Billy Bob brought a cup of his dad's 'afternoon tea' and they sat there and drank it and both became dizzy from the effects the homemade alcohol had on them. This led to kissing and hugging, and on the fateful day when Betty Jane was nineteen and Billy Bob was twenty-one, they went too far and Betty Jane had become pregnant. She and Billy Bob talked about what to do, both too scared to tell anyone, and finally they agreed that after telling their parents, they would go to Carter and get married.

Neither one told their parents as they had planned. Both were too scared. Betty Jane started getting sick in the mornings and tried to hide it from her family. Billy Bob kept going to 'their place' and would write notes and leave them for Betty Jane. But since she never went there anymore, she never knew. He was afraid to go to her house so several weeks went by without them knowing what the other was thinking.

*****

Betty Jane arrived at Billy Bob's house and knocked on the door. When his mother answered, she was surprised to see Betty Jane standing there.

"I thought you were with Billy Bob! When he left here early this morning, he said he was going to get you and you were going to Carter to get married. Has something happened? He's been so upset lately, saying something like you never gave him any answers, or didn't seem to care, or something like that. But when he left, he was in high spirits and said he was to meet you someplace away from your house since your parents didn't approve of the marriage. His pa and I think you would make a wonderful couple so we gave him our blessing. I planned to go talk to your daddy today about it to see if I could change his mind about the wedding."

Betty Jane was shocked! She was surprised! Did she have a feeling of joy? Of relief? There was warmth between Betty Jane and Billy Bob's mother, Fanny. They had often gone blackberry picking together and made jam for both families. They would sit on the back porch at Billy Bob's and talk of what was going to happen in the valley, of plans they both had and Fanny taught Betty Jane how to sew and cook. Annie was not able to do much work and ma was busy doing other things so Betty Jane spent a lot of time with Fanny.

Fanny thought she should go with Betty Jane to see if Billy Bob might be at Betty Jane's house. She put on her bonnet, took a basket of apples for ma, and they left.

*****

Billy Bob had been hesitant to tell his parents. He knew they liked Betty Jane but he also knew they had plans for him to go to college, as his mother put it, 'To make a name for yourself.' This, of course, would delay his leaving, if he ever got to go.

When he did tell them, they were disappointed but happy for him to be marrying Betty Jane.

"Son, maybe we can work something out and you can go to college anyway. We'll talk with Benny and see what he might think. You go on and do right by Betty Jane. You marry her and you can move in here until you can decide what you want to do. There's always a place for you here on the farm."

Billy Bob left for Betty Jane's and on the way, he went up to their 'cave' and left a note for Betty Jane. He knew she didn't go there anymore but someday she would go and his note would be there for her to read. Maybe they would go together after they were married. He left it by a rock where it would be easy for her to find. On his way to her house, he thought he would ask Junior to go with them to be the best man and they would let the Reverend Clark do the wedding.

He was close to her house when he heard someone call to him.

"Hey, Billy Bob. I hear you want to marry my little sister."

He looked into the woods and saw Johnny standing behind a large beech tree. Being a little worried, thinking Johnny might have been drinking, but also thinking Junior was probably with Johnny, he called back, "That's right. She sure is a wonderful woman."

Johnny came up to him and said, "She sure is, or was, until you did what you did."

"Now wait a minute, Johnny. I'm going to marry her and make it right. I want to marry her anyway and Junior knows that, don't you, Junior?"

Calling out to Junior, and hoping he was there, he heard no answer.

"Junior ain't around, boy. This is just between you and me. You've damaged my sister and you have me to answer to."

With that, Johnny hit Billy Bob and knocked him to the ground. Johnny was much bigger and stronger and Billy Bob tried to talk to him but to no avail. Johnny hit him several times, cutting his face and knocking the wind out of him.

"Now listen here, Mr. Billy Bob Kryster. You're leaving this valley and you're leaving now, and you ain't coming back, ever. Hear me, boy? Hear me?"

He picked Billy Bob up and put him on a spare horse he had hidden in the woods, and they both rode out of the valley, taking the back trails so they wouldn't be seen.

They arrived at the train depot in Olive Hill some hours later, where Johnny bought a one-way ticket for Billy Bob to Cincinnati.

"That ticket took all my money and I consider it well spent, to get rid of trash like you. Don't you ever show up here again and don't you ever try to write to anyone."

With that, he put Billy Bob on the train and stood there until it pulled out of the station.

When Fanny and Betty Jane arrived at Benny's, they were told that Billy Bob had never been there. Worried, they began searching the roads, and Junior rode into Carter to see if he had been there. No one had seen him. After several days of searching, they had assumed he had been too scared to go through with the wedding and had run off. Johnny had told them he had not seen him around Olive Hill, while he was there getting some supplies.

No one ever heard from Billy Bob again. Annie unaware of the problem, died soon after Billy Bob disappeared. Life resumed on the Creek at the normal pace and Betty Jane soon had a baby boy. A fine healthy son and with the baby, came a mingling of joy and sadness for Betty Jane. With the help and support of her family, she stayed home and took care of Benny and Junior. Ma and pa passed away after a few years; Fanny died of a broken heart over losing Billy Bob, and Johnny left home soon after the baby was born. Betty Jane never married and her son, Tony, grew into a fine young man, helping out on the farm and when he finished high school, he was able to attend a nearby college and eventually became an attorney.

A tradition of homecoming had begun on the Creek and one August day, many years later, about one hundred people gathered at the old school house to hear the now aging Reverend Clark, give a sermon, and then share in food spread out on tables over the grounds. The preacher talked about 'coming home' and how this gathering could compare to 'coming home to Jesus." Betty Jane had helped prepare food and Tony had helped set up the tables. Instead of going to the church service in the morning, she had made a decision that would change her life forever. She went to the 'cave' where she and Billy Bob had spent so many hours.

Tony greeted the people as they came out of the service, directing them to the tables and food. One man, a tall distinguished looking gentleman, shook Tony's hand and asked him if he had ever heard of a Betty Jane McGlone.

"Why, yes sir. She's my mother. Would you like to meet her? Oh, I forgot. She isn't here at the moment. Said she was going to some secret place that I could never know about. She should be back sometime soon. You go ahead and eat and I'll let you know when she returns."

Slipping away from everyone, the man walked up the nearby hillside and as he approached the 'cave,' he was careful not to make any noise. Betty Jane was standing just outside the entrance reading some notes. He watched her carefully as she placed them back where she found them, and then she took an envelope out of her pocket, placed it with the other notes, and walked away.

As she moved around the pocket of brush, the man walked to the entrance, removed the notes, noticed the new one, and stopped to read it.

A flower had bloomed, an egg had hatched, and a bird was born. The lord and lady of the forest, a buck and a doe, watched their newborn play among the grass.
They were safe because-----YOU WERE THERE.

A bird chirped, and off in the woods, a squirrel played among the giant oaks.
A turkey strutted across the dew-laden lawn.
They too, were safe because------
YOU WERE THERE.

Off over the big hill, God's paintbrush painted the morning sky with its reds and yellows. The gentle breezes blew the soft, puffy clouds slowly across the Heavens. ---There was no hurry because-----
---YOU WERE THERE.

The morning star rose high in the sky sending its rays of warmth to wash away the chills of the night. The yellow butterfly flew among the flowers, as a hummingbird hovered over its morning meal. There was peace because----
YOU WERE THERE.

A friend waved. Love, happiness and peace floated on the easy breezes; calmness settled over the land. There was no problem because-------
YOU WERE THERE.

The sun ends its journey of the day, painting once again the evening sky with the colors of God's rainbow. Now only a tiny dot, sinking slowly into the far distant horizon, the cooling wind of the evening blows across the land, a land of peace, Because-------YOU WERE THERE.

The great moon rises in its fullness –driving away the twinkling of the stars—lighting up the land as though it were still day. Then, it too, surrenders to the glory of another day.
God's hand is at work in the world because---- YOU WERE THERE.

Now, great peals of thunder and brilliant flashes of lightning light up the sky, blocking out the morning star. A raindrop fell or was it a tear? There was sadness upon the Creek. You see-----
---YOU WERE GONE.

Goodbye, Billy Bob Kryster. I loved you and I still do. May you know wherever you are, the peace of many more happy years.

*****

Billy Bob read the note Betty Jane had left. Hurrying to catch her before she left the ridge, he called out to her. He had not heard her return to the 'cave.' She had heard someone approaching and came back to see who had found the spot, held in secret for so many years.

"Billy Bob? Is that you?"

Betty Jane wanted to run to him, yet, she held back thinking it might be an intruder.

Years had been kind to both of them. Billy Bob had been a successful businessman in Ohio and Betty Jane had retained her beauty. Unbelieving, but still knowing, they sat there on the hillside, laughing, crying and telling each other their stories. The afternoon passed quickly by as they declared their ongoing, everlasting love for one another. Billy Bob had never married, often thinking he would come back to the Creek to get her, but afraid of finding her married to another. He was no longer afraid of Johnny and had no comment when she told him Johnny had been killed in an automobile accident.

Betty Jane heard Tony calling for her and as they walked away from the 'secret spot' for the last time, they mourned the wasted years they had lost because of fear. Hand in hand and arm in arm, they walked off into the sunset with hope for their future together.

THE STORM

A feeling of sadness seemed to be borne by the wind as it blew harder and harder up the little valley. Tree branches bent with the sudden gusts, little waves on the not too deep waters of the creek, rippled toward the brush-lined shore. Deep, dark clouds raced across the darkening sky, broken only occasionally by rays of the sun as it struggled to keep the light of the day. The whispering wind sounded like ghosts come to haunt the few residents of the valley. Ghosts of the past--but what past? These twenty-eight people were the only present residents of the Creek and as far as anyone knew, very few had ever lived there before, not even Indians.

So, I listened to the wind. Listened to its sighing among the trees, and I made my way up the valley to the little church. As I rode along the narrow dirt road, I could hear whispers deep within my soul.

Passing my sister's home, I saw her standing out by the well getting ready to draw some water. "Hey, Sis." She waved at me and motioned for me to come on in. "I can't now. I'm on my way to church. You're not going today, huh?"

"No. Eddie's feeling poorly today and we decided it best we stay home. He just got back from Grayson where he picked up some iron bars to make that fence for George Watson over at Carter. Said the wagon broke down twice and it took him all week to go there and get back. I think he got too hot and then cooled off too fast." Sis had walked out to the road to talk with me. Eddie was the only blacksmith in the area and they were thinking of moving to nearby Carter where he could be closer to his business.

"I know ma and pa will be unhappy to see us leave here but the ride to Carter and back every day is too much for Eddie. We've found us a nice place to live and as soon as Eddie is well, we're going to move. I'll be up this week to see ma and pa. You tell them hello for me and I'll be there for sure."

"Maybe you're right, Sis. I think it's a good idea and you two need to do what you think is best. I know ma will want you to stay but pa will go along with what you think is the proper thing to do. Best I go on now. I'm a bit late as it is. Say hey to Eddie for me."

I hurried 'ol Tom along and soon I could hear the singing of a new song, "BRING THEM IN-----" coming from the whitewashed building. I was there to share with others who had come to the late afternoon services held by a visiting preacher. Pa had built a crude building and the neighbors joined in and gave it a finish of whitewash. Some of the whitewash had washed off in the rains but we did have a place to meet and worship once a month when the preacher could come to meet with us. He held a morning service in Carter, about six miles away, and then he rode his horse up on the Creek to hold the afternoon service for us. Most of the folks turned out for the service as it was the only time we could all get together and forget for a moment the heavy burden placed upon us to settle the valley.

The people were all part of Mark's clan and most had stayed here to farm the little tracts of land left to them by Mark at his death just a few weeks ago. Grandpa Mark had settled here with grandma and their five children about 1810. Now there were twenty-eight people, seven families including ours.   Only one other family had moved in and that was Jeremiah Gilson and his wife, Ibella. Jeremiah had come to the Creek about four years ago and asked Grandpa Mark if he could purchase a small tract of land up on Garvin Ridge, named after my oldest uncle, Garvin. The land was almost worthless but Jeremiah had said he was a simple man and didn't want much. Just a place to grow some corn, have him a little garden, and a place to be alone. Said he had a couple of hogs and some cows with a horse or two. Grandpa didn't want the land and none of the children wanted it either, so he sold it to Jeremiah for fifteen dollars with the understanding that Jeremiah would not trespass on any of Mark's lands, to hunt or to farm. Jeremiah said he would make him a road down the other side of the ridge and would not even come down into Mark's valley. He kept his word for all those months, the only exception was when Ibella came to church services, and no one objected to that.

We soon found Ibella stuttered something awful when she tried to talk so she seldom spoke to anyone when she was in church. Just nodded her head and sat down and when the service was almost over, she would get up and leave. One Sunday afternoon when ma and pa were on the way to the church house to get it ready for the afternoon services, they heard a beautiful voice off in the woods singing 'TIS SO SWEET TO TRUST IN JESUS. Soon Ibella emerged from the trees and saw ma and pa. Startled, she ran back into the woods and acted like she didn't want to be seen. Pa caught up with her, asked if that was her singing. She nodded her head, and tried to pull away.

"But girl, you stutter all the time. Do you mean to tell me you can sing like that without the stutter?"

"Ye ye ye ye s sir." She stammered out. Making pa understand that she didn't stutter when she sang was hard for her but he finally realized her problem.

"Sing for us today, Ibella. Sing your heart out. Let us hear the glory of God in your voice. That's the prettiest voice I've ever heard."

When the service started and the preacher announced the first hymn, Pa stood up and said he had a surprise and if the preacher didn't mind, he would like to have a solo sung.

"Now folks, this song is called 'TIS SO SWEET TO TRUST IN JESUS, and it is sung by as beautiful voice as you will ever hear. Listen carefully."

Everyone looked around to see who was going to do the singing and they laughed when Ibella shyly got up and walked to the front of the little building. Ma gave her a note on the mouth organ and she began singing. No one moved, even after the song was finished, no one said anything, stunned into silence by her voice. The preacher stood up, walked over to Ibella, "Woman, God has spoken to us today with your voice. You're His angel come to bless us." Tears flowed down his cheeks as he led her to a seat up front.

After that, most every time the preacher came to us, he had Ibella sing at least one hymn. Time passed and the visits Ibella made to us grew fewer and fewer. One Sunday she came but it was obvious something was wrong with her. She limped and had her left eye covered with a patch. She wouldn't sing or talk to anyone.

Before the service was over, she got up and left. No more was heard from Ibella. Pa often thought he should go up on the ridge to see if everything was all right but ma told him not to interfere. "If they need us, they will come to us."

"Now, Ma, I've got me a feeling. I don't rightly think I like what I've been seeing when Ibella is around. I think maybe Jeremiah has something to do with her condition. I certainly hope he isn't abusing her but I'm a little concerned. I don't think I like it, Ma."

"Well, I don't think I like it either but what is happening is between them and I don't think we should interfere. Maybe I can talk to her next time she comes around."

But she never came again.

*****

"Howdy boys." Cousin Alfred and three or four men were standing around outside as I rode up.

"You fellers not going to the service today?"

They mostly nodded to me and I noticed a stranger among them but thought nothing of it at the time. I was a little late for the service and as I went into the building, thunder could be heard over the hills and an occasional streak of lightning could be seen. The preacher was well into his sermon when Alfred came into the building, spoke out quite loudly, saying, "Preacher, I'm sorry to bother you, but it appears like we're going to get some kind of a storm. Some of us have a ways to go and maybe you should stop the service so we can get home before the rains come. It looks bad out here." Those of us in the church had heard the thunder and saw the lightning flashes and I guess we were a bit antsy sitting there trying to listen to the preacher and wondering when the rain would come.

"Brother Alfred, you may be right. I do believe the Lord is speaking to us so I'll have a prayer and we will all go home. I have a long way to go today so I'll end the service here. You folks remember the Lord cares for you and if you noticed, He had Brother Jeremiah come visit us today. He wouldn't come inside but he was here and that's a start. I wish he would have brought Ibella with him but he says she is poorly and was not able to come."

The preacher had a short prayer, which was a rarity for him and everyone said goodbye and began hurrying home. Some of the men standing outside seemed to be staggering a little and that's when pa found out Jeremiah, who was the stranger I had seen, had been giving them some of his 'shine he had made back upon the ridge.

"So that's how he managed to live." Pa was a little more than upset at that discovery. "I'll have to talk to him this week. We can't have that here on the Creek. And I'm going to talk with him about Ibella."

"You do that, Pa. But you take a couple of the boys with you. That Jeremiah may mean trouble and we don't want that."

As we hurried to our homes, sprinkles began but they were not hard enough to keep us from doing the evening chores. Nothing really ever stopped the evening chores! Cows had to be milked, hogs needed to be fed, meals had to be cooked. Since this was mid-August, daylight lingered long into the evening.

So, even with the raging clouds, light still stayed with us. I helped ma with the preparation of supper, carrying in water, setting the table, and so on. Usually we would sit on the porch after the evening meal listening to the frogs sing to us, and soon, off on the tree-lined ridge, the whippoorwill took up its lonely cry. Bats would dart overhead as insects filled the wind-blown night air. And on these warm evenings, honeysuckle would spread its aroma through the meadows. Sometimes a visitor would come by and visit awhile.   Some of the young boys, myself included, would often ride over to Carter to do some courting with the young girls there. Everyone here in the valley was related so we had to go elsewhere to do our matchmaking. And a few of the men from Carter and surrounding areas would come up on the Creek to visit our women.

But not this night! An eerie stillness settled over the valley. A feeling was in the air—the whispering hills gave up a feeling of rain and all of us settled down with the windows open to catch the cool night breezes.

The rain began in earnest just after dark. It rained hard all night and kept it up all next day. A hard rain, a consistent rain. The creek started to fill up and the washes down the sides of the hills were overflowing. The third day came and still no let up in the rain. We had to go out to the barn and check to see that the animals were doing all right. The chicken house leaked rather badly and pa thought maybe we should put the chickens in the big barn.

At noon of the third day, we heard a shout and it was Cousin Arthur coming across the hill back of the house.

"I'm being flooded out. The creek is overflowing and is right at the edge of my house. In fact, when I left, it was coming into the kitchen. We have to move to higher ground and there is no place to go. Mabel is crying and I don't know what to do. Maybe she could come over here? I don't think you'll have any trouble since you are so high off the creek floor. If you stand up there on the hill, you can see that the whole valley is flooded and it's going to get worse. Gerald's house, and Marty's and Kenneth's, are already being covered with water and I saw someone on the other side of the valley headed for high ground. I didn't check on Eddie's and Harry's. They may be in trouble because Eddie is definitely in line with the water.

Pa told him to go get Mabel and she could stay here. Saying to me, "Maybe we should go look around and see if we can help anybody. That water is a raging torrent now and I expect there is a lot of trouble all up and down the Creek. But let's go look after the animals first."

"Hey, Pa. Look down there. That's somebody's shed floating down the water. I think you're right. We had best look over the valley. I'm afraid we have some problems on our hands. I can't believe this much water can be in the valley. We may have to take the animals out of the barn and put them up behind the house in the pasture up there. It looks like the barn will be flooded if the rain doesn't stop. The whole valley floor looks to be flooded. Where do you want to go first?"

"Let's go get the animals. We had best do it now before nightfall. We may not have a barn in the morning and we can't afford to lose the animals." Our farm was the center part of the valley. Grandpa Mark had given pa this farm and it was considered the best farm around. Pa had worked hard and it was in good shape. It sat between two hills and was higher than the farmland around us. There would be no worry about our house being flooded but no one else was that fortunate. When we got back to the house, we found six of our cousins and their families at our house. They had no place else to go except up into the hills and ma would have no part of that. We would sleep on the floors and in the attic and anywhere else that we had to. Two more people had just come in so we were filling up fast. Most of them had lost their homes and barns and many of the animals. However, some had let their animals loose and most of them wandered up into the hills and they could be rounded up later. As far as we knew, no one had drowned. Pa and some of the men went down the valley hugging the side of the hills and some others and me went the other way.

On the night of the fourth day, the rain stopped as suddenly as it had begun. Next morning, the sun was shining brightly on a valley still flooded and devastated. Nothing was left intact. Barns were gone. We were fortunate; ours only had water standing in it. Two houses had washed away against some trees down stream and three more had water in them up to the windows. We couldn't get close enough to any of them to see about the damage done. Finally the rivers down from the valley had been able to handle the overflow and our creek began to recede. Everyone was accounted for so we were fortunate there, but the loss of property was maybe beyond recovery. Crops were washed away and the real problem of food for the coming winter was with us. Pa had said we needed to sit down with everyone and do some planning for the future. Some even said they were going to leave the valley. Sis and Eddie had showed up and said they were definitely going.

Our little church house was gone and Pa thought we ought to go up on Garvin Ridge to see how Jeremiah and Ibella had done in the rainstorm.

When we arrived, we saw their little house, or rather, shack, was washed over the side of the hill. The supports holding it up had given way and it just collapsed. We looked for both of them and pa called to me to come help him. He had found Jeremiah pinned under the collapsed porch and had been dead for some time. I found an old shovel and dug a grave and marked it for Ibella to see when we found her. We just put his remains in the grave and covered them up. There was no time for a coffin to be made. We looked and looked and never did find Ibella. Later, down in

Carter, they found some bodies in the river, and they couldn't be identified. One was a woman. Whether it was Ibella or not, we never found out. They buried them at once because of the smell of the human flesh. How she got that far down the creek, we didn't know although the water current was certainly strong enough to carry her there. She may have fallen into the hillside wash of water and down into the creek and was just carried away.

Soon after the flood, some folks left the valley but ma and pa wanted no part of it. They bought some of the land and in later years, became rather prosperous farmers.

I, too, left the valley. One morning in early spring, I said goodbye to my family, tears falling down my cheeks, and rode away. I never looked back that day and never went back until I was an old man, maybe fifty years after I had left. Of course, ma and pa were gone along with many of my family. I had gone up north to Michigan where I did quite well in the timber business and became too busy to go "home." The day I did go back, I stopped and looked up the Creek, saw visions of lovely people working the land, good hard honest people. Sure, some were still there, still working hard, still making a living, still enjoying the gift of God. And here I stood. What do I have? Money? Sure! Plenty of money. But what do I really have? I have faith in our Maker and with deep gratitude that He let me return to my "home", to do some good before I depart this cruel world.

Memories? I have beautiful memories. Beautiful dreams of days gone by, and these dreams and memories fill my soul. There, off in the meadows, a bobwhite sang its final song of the day. And up there in the valley, there is a peaceful little creek, flowing sometimes, but mostly mere puddles. But peace there is. There is lots of love, friends, good times with simple folks, all living out their lives with faith in the Lord. The winds blow, but there is no sadness, only warm gentle winds telling me "welcome home." I look into the Heavens and see a world far apart from what I have been accustomed to. I saw a puffy white cloud moving across a sunlit sky, I saw a bluebird make a nest in a box on a fence, I saw

a newborn calf following its mother, I saw the Lord reach down and touch me with His love and I am content...
I AM HOME!

FAREWELL TO THE CREEK

I left home in the year nineteen hundred and two.   I didn't like the farm work, I didn't like the school work, so I guess I thought I could go to the far ends of the world, make a success of myself, and come back to the Creek and show everyone what I had done.

I did go to the far ends of the world but not as I had planned. I went to Norfolk, Virginia, and found a man who talked me into becoming a sailor. With the bright picture he painted, I imagined the romance of sailing the seas, the fortune awaiting me, so I agreed and signed on the good ship, Philantia, and became a sailor. Sailing into a small port in Greece, I was enticed into staying by a young Greek maiden who promised me the Fruits of Paradise. The fruits quickly turned into working on her father's olive ranch, and disillusioned, I left on the next ship where I could find a berth.

As I sailed the oceans, World War One soon came along, and back in America, I joined the Navy. I found I could use my knowledge of the sea, and soon was given a commission. Moving troops across the North Atlantic to Europe was a cold, hard experience and dodging the German Navy ships, I found my yearning for travel and adventure was being turned into a desire for the peace and quiet of my youthful country living.

The war ended and the troops had to come home. While escorting a troop ship back to the United States, I met a young soldier, an officer in the Infantry, who asked me to join him in a business venture after our tours of duty ended. It sounded promising so I agreed to meet him at his home in Michigan. I was released from the Navy in nineteen twenty three and made my way across the eastern United States to Michigan where I looked up Robert Ernest, the man I had met on the way home from Europe.

Together, we pooled our meager resources we had accumulated from the service, and formed a construction company to build roads, much needed across the nation. We worked hard for five years, building roads all over the mid west. Our business grew rapidly and we saw nothing but success upon the horizon. In nineteen twenty-eight, late in the year, I was sitting in my office in Detroit, when I received a telegram asking me to come to Ohio as quickly as possible. My partner, Robert, had been killed in an accident when a bulldozer turned over on him.

Arriving two days later, I found that he had been trying to run a bulldozer up a steep bank and it had turned over on him and pinned him beneath one of the tracks. I had him transported back to his home in Detroit and attended the funeral with his family.

One week after the accident, I was approached by a group of businessmen in Detroit wanting to buy the business. Still feeling wretched from losing my partner, I agreed to a financial settlement, much in my favor. They wanted to pay me over a period of five years but I insisted on cash, giving them a break on the selling price, which they finally agreed to. My partner and I had an agreement that if either of us died, the surviving family would get one half of the selling price if the business was sold.

I was born in eighteen eighty and it was now nineteen twenty eight, so at forty eight, I decided I had enough money to support me for the rest of my life and thought it best I begin to see parts of the world I still had a yen to visit.

I had cashed the check, put the money in the bank, and later decided to withdraw it and put it in my safe at home. I had heard rumors that the economics of the country was in trouble and a banker friend of mine had suggested I be a bit cautious with where

I put my money. Not really realizing how much I had, I created quite a stir at the bank when I withdrew all but a few thousand dollars.

Four days later, the crash came! I lost most of the three thousand dollars I had left in the bank but I had my cash safely in my safe at home. I think to this day that the Lord guided me. I had always been a religious man, even as I roamed the seas. My mother had raised a large family and we faithfully attended the little church just up the road from our home on the Creek. None of this training was lost on me as I grew up, not that I attended church regularly, not even when I was ashore, but the memory of the advice from mother stayed with me in my soul.

I used my money sparingly, living well, but not in an ostentatious manner. I lived in Detroit for several years, but one day, in the year nineteen forty-one, I decided to go back to the Creek to see if any of my family still were living. This is the one thing that haunted me through the years. I had lost all contact with my family. Mother had died before I left home and father was not well. Some of my brothers had stayed on the farm but others had gone away to Arizona to the copper mines, to Oregon to the lumber mills, and the sisters were getting married. Home as I once knew it, no longer existed.

Maybe the war had created an emotionalism within me. Maybe the loss of my partner had caused me to think of life as it was passing by. Something happened! I was now in my sixties and all of a sudden, I felt the haunting winds of so many years ago, and left for a visit to the Creek. Were my brothers still there? Would I know anyone? My girl friend, when I was a teenager, would be married by now with a family of her own but I wanted to see her. I remember leaving her a note saying only, "We're parting but someday you'll understand." Would I be welcomed back?

Another war had begun. I knew that there would be a shortage of working folk and I could apply for a job, or buy a company, or do most anything to help the nation in its time of need. No! I didn't want that. I was patriotic but time was passing me by and I needed to see what the past had left for me.

So—days later, as I sat there looking up the valley, I could hear the mournful cry of the winds as the spirits of those long gone, moved over the hills. I knew mother had gone and I'm sure father had passed on shortly after I had left home. But there were brothers and sisters and nephews and nieces to visit. What would I find?

Driving slowly up the lonely narrow, dusty road, I remembered most every house. Maybe one or two were new but not many. I knew life on the Creek had not been easy; it never would be. Some corn, tobacco, cattle, and a few hogs were all the farmers could raise, plus the little gardens, which supplied so much of the foodstuff, needed over the winter months.

The house was there! A front porch had been added and it was now painted white instead of the whitewash used earlier. The barn was across the road and the apple orchard, if one could call it an orchard, was still located near the barn. There was a new outhouse sitting back up the path from the house and the old cellar was still there. Not much had changed!

I parked the car and started to walk up to the house when two young children came racing around the corner with a June bug tied to a string and almost bumped into me.

"I'm sorry, Mister. I sure didn't see you. Are you here to see my pa?"

"I believe that's true, young man. And don't you worry about almost bumping into me. I'll bet you I can make that June bug move faster than you can."

"I'll catch another and we'll have a race." The young lad raced back around the house just as a pretty young woman came out the door.

"Howdy, ma'am. I just bet your boy there that I could beat him in a June bug race. Sorry. I was not intending to intrude but we just happened to meet as I was coming to the door."

"That's quite all right. I'm Judy Masterson. My husband is Elroy. That's him coming up from the barn. Can we help you with something?"

Walking over to meet Elroy, I said, "Elroy, my name is Win Masterson. Somewhere along the line, I think we're related. I used to live here, in fact, I was born here, in that room just over the new porch." "You must be Uncle Win. I've heard many tales about you but we thought you were probably dead, since we hadn't heard from you for years. Come on up to the porch and we can visit. Judy, do you have any cool buttermilk ready?"

I sat down in the rocker, Judy got the buttermilk, came back and sat in the swing, and Elroy sat upon the banister of the porch, leaning back against a post. The young boy came running back with a June bug and asked if I was going to race him. Elroy spoke up, "Lonnie, can you wait until later? We're going to have a talk with Uncle Win. Uncle Win, this is our only son, Lonnie. We have a daughter but she's up the Creek visiting with her aunt."

"All right, Pa. But I bet Win, er, Uncle Win, that I can beat him. Can I look at your car, Uncle Win? I ain't never seen one that purty before."

Judy spoke up. "You mean 'you've never seen one that pretty before,' don't you, Lonnie?"

"Yessum, Ma. That's what I mean."

Win nodded for him to go ahead and racing over to the car, he looked it over carefully.

"Maybe we can all go for a ride if it's all right with your parents, Lonnie."

Before I got an answer, a wagon slowly moved past the old house, where I was sitting with Elroy and Judy.

"Howdy!" A deep voice called out to Elroy and Elroy waved back and invited the man and woman in for a rest.

"Cain't make hit terday, thankee. Me and Idy Mae here air goin' inter Carter ta get us some vittles. Idy Mae wants to make some berry jam and needs some sugar and spices. Guess we'll be goin' on our way."

Ida Mae sat there on the wagon seat and peered toward the porch; in her toothless mouth she had her corncob pipe and moved it up and down as she breathed. It wasn't lit and Judy said Ida never seemed to smoke it. Cackling in her nasal voice, "Vincent! Hit's him! Hit's Billy Joe fer shore! Lookee yonder. Hit's him! Howdee, Billy Joe! Hit's me, Idy Mae. You still be awaitin' fer me? Well, I'm married to Vincent now and he's my man fer shore."

Vincent turned to Ida Mae. "Shet yore mouth, Idy. You know that ain't Billy Joe. Billy Joe's been dead nigh onto twenty years. Yore mind is wanderin' agin. Now sit down and we'll get moving."

Ida Mae sat down but called out once more. "Billy Joe, you wanted me back then and I know you still do, but you cain't. I'm married now."

Vincent called out an apology to Elroy and said, "Idy be a gettin' a little worse. She's living out her childhood." With that, he moved on down the road in the wagon.

"What was that all about, Elroy? Who was that?"

"Win, that old woman is about to lose it all. She thought you were Grandpa Billy Joe. Guess at one time grandpa had a crush on her or so she always says. You do look a little like him, you know."

They talked another few minutes and Elroy said he had best go tend to the afternoon chores. I said I would go help but Elroy said he could handle them.

"You sit right there and when I get back, we'll have us a big supper.

I sat there in the rocker looking out over the farm where I had grown up. Rocking back and forth with my mind on my earlier days here on the farm, I didn't hear Judy walk up. Startled, I stood up.

"I'm sorry. I guess I must have been lost in thought. I didn't even hear you coming."

"That's quite all right, Win. I talked with Elroy down at the barn and we both want you to stay with us for a few days. He wants to talk about family and what has happened to all of them, and also, little Lonnie says you must have that race with him."

"I'm afraid my staying would be too much of a burden to you. I can go into town and get a room and come back later."

"Don't you even think that, Win Masterson. You're just like the rest of the men were. Stubborn as you can be. You will stay right here with us. We have plenty of room and we want you to stay.

"All right, I'll stay."

Laughing, I said, "I'm going to get Lonnie and have that race. Maybe we can walk down by the creek. I used to have a favorite place down there where I would hide from ma when she called me. Oh, she always knew where I was but pretended she couldn't find me. We had lots of fun while I was growing up."

Judy called out to Lonnie and he came running with his June bug. "I'll get you one, Uncle Win. Wait right here."

Lonnie raced back and off we went to race our bugs. I soon gave out and called to Lonnie that he had won and he would get the prize.

"As soon as we get back to the house, I'll get you the prize. I'll have to ask your ma and pa if it's all right with them."

We walked back toward the house along the now brush overgrown creek bank and when we came to the spot where I used to play, I told Lonnie that I used to hide there when I was little. "My mother always found me but she would pretend I had hidden from her for a long time. It was a fun game we played."

At supper that night, Elroy told me what had happened to my family.

"Your father died soon after you left. He never knew you had gone. I guess his mind had completely gone after your mother died, or so dad told me. Dad had a heart attack when I was twenty-two and Judy and I got married a year later. Dad left the farm to me since I was the only one who cared to stay. Now it looks like

I may have to go to the army although I don't see real well out of my left eye. As soon as we can afford it, I'm going to get some glasses. We don't have a lot of money here on the farm, Win, but we have a good life and I wouldn't trade it for anything. I don't know what will happen to Judy if I'm drafted but I'm sure she will get by. There's a young boy up the road who said he would help her if needed."

Elsie came racing in for supper crying out, "I hope I'm not too late!"

That drew a stern look from Judy.

"I agreed to stay for a few days if they would let me help with some of the odd jobs. "I'm afraid I'm not in shape for much hard work but I'll do what I can to help. I promised Lonnie a prize for winning the race and if you don't mind, I'd like to take him into town tomorrow and get him a bicycle. You can tell him it's a birthday present from me if you wish. He told me his birthday is next week. Elroy, I'm not trying to interfere with your family. I would like very much to do this for Lonnie and then there's Elsie. I'll tell you what! Why don't we all go to town tomorrow! Yes, let's do that.   We'll make it a vacation day. What do you say , Niece Judy? Talk your husband into the day off."

"Oh, I'm afraid there is too much to do here. Milking has to be done, feeding has to be done, and plowing has to be done. There's too much to do."

"Come on, Elroy. One day won't hurt."

"Please, Father. Just for one day. We haven't been to town for a long time." Elsie was pleading with Elroy and he finally consented.

"You know we can't buy anything now. We have to wait until the crops are in." Embarrassed, he looked at Win and began to apologize. "We don't have the money right now, Uncle Win. We'll get them all something later."

"Elroy, let's me and you take a walk down to the barn to see the animals. I'm still part farmer you know. I'd like to see around the place a bit. Lonnie, you'll have to stay here this time. I want to talk with your dad. Judy, would you like to go along?"

"Do you mind? Elroy, is it all right with you?"

"Sure. You come along with us. It will be more fun than talking with the children all the time. You come right ahead." Telling the children to stay near the house, the three of them walked off.

"Elroy and Judy, I need to say something to you but am not sure how to say it. If I hurt your feelings in any way, I apologize now. I'm going to go ahead and say it and you can do with it as you please."

Walking slowly and pointing toward the nearby meadow, "I used to play down there under that big oak tree. Dad made us a swing and we had a big time trying to outdo the others. You know of course, that I was the youngest and usually got the last turn." Laughing, I paused for a bit, then walked on.

"Elroy, you and Judy work hard here on the farm. It's no disgrace to have little or no money."

I was embarrassed and didn't know just how to say it and I stuttered a little and then went on. "I'm not a rich man but I do have plenty, perhaps more than I'll ever need. What I'm trying to say is, let me help you out a little and someday if you can, you can pay me back, but I don't want you to worry about it. I left my family here and they had nothing then. I guess I was fortunate in making a lot of money and more fortunate yet, I didn't lose much in the depression. For some reason, I felt that I had to come back here to the Creek and now I feel that I want to help you two and the children. Now don't take this wrong. I would be honored to help you and I feel you are family and I feel I owe it to you, now my only family, to make amends for not helping out a long time ago. And, you're the only family I have left, or that I know about. How about it? Will you let me help? Please?"

Judy started crying. "Uncle Win, we're not desperate. We can make it on our own and we are trying hard to do so. You're so kind. Here you are, someone who just happened to drive up to our home and now you want to help us. I guess I don't understand. Why do you want to do that?"

"Judy, I don't know why other than the reason I gave you. Maybe the Lord spoke to me and told me to do something to help someone and maybe He led me back here, back to my old home. I don't know, Judy. That's all I can say about it. Will you let me help you? I know you can make it on your own by working all the time and never enjoying life as you should. And the children; they are lovely kids. Let's just be a family again and you welcome me back and I'll enjoy myself for the short time I can stay. I'll even come back often if you will let me?"

Elroy had said nothing. He moved over close to Judy, took her hand and said softly, "Judy, maybe this is what we have been praying for."

Looking at me, he said, "Win, I pray every night that I can make life easier for Judy and the children. They are such wonderful people and I feel I owe them so much more than I have given them. We'll accept your offer on one condition and that is that you come back here as often as you can. I'll give you some farm work to do, and we will indeed be a big happy family again. We'll take your offer as a loan and try hard to pay you back someday."

Elroy put his arm around Judy and said, "Now, we're going to town tomorrow, you can get the children bicycles, and we're going to come home and have a big feast. Even a celebration! No, we won't do it tomorrow. We will do it Sunday after church and invite some friends in and have them meet you, Win. You will stay awhile, won't you?"

"I had planned to leave on Saturday morning but I believe I can stretch it out until Monday if you can manage me that long."

Laughing and talking, the three of us continued on our walk.

Early next morning, Elroy finished milking, and did some other minor farm chores and then we all piled in the car and headed to town. Most of the folks had never seen a car as fine as this one so we got a lot of attention as we drove down the main street of town. The kids were kept busy waving to friends.

Shopping was done, bicycles were bought to the whooping and crying of the kids, and just before we were to leave for home, I took Elroy by the arm and herded him into the doctor's office where he had his eyes checked, and new glasses were ordered and to be delivered by mail when they were ready.

I stayed past Monday; I didn't leave until the next weekend. Promising to come back for Thanksgiving and even Christmas, I waved goodbye to my new found family and slowly drove off. Sometime when Judy stripped the bed, I hoped, as she pulled back the sheets, she would find a large amount of money under them and a little note in which I merely said, "I love you all." And I had signed it," Uncle Win."

I slowly drove down the dusty road. I stopped at a curve in the road near the creek and decided to take a short walk around the hillside. I had played there as a youngster and as I sat on the moss covered ground, I could see smoke coming from the chimney of Maurie's house. Maurie had been my childhood sweetheart and Elroy had told me she had four children and was happily married. Roosters were crowing and an occasional cow would send out her moos as woodland silence permeated the valley. A man was plowing in the distance and I assumed it was Maurie's husband.

Why would pa want to stay here and farm? I sat and thought about the valley as it once may have been. There's lots of good farmland elsewhere but not much here on the Creek. I wish I had asked him but I guess he found pleasure in settling here.

I had to go. Getting back into the car I sat still for a moment, then drove away in a cloud of dust.

*****

Nothing more was heard from or about Win until late next spring. A large automobile moved up to the house, a distinguished looking gentleman got out of the car, and introduced himself as William Cookhouse, Attorney.

"Mr. and Mrs. Masterson, I represent the estate of Win Masterson.   Mr. Masterson passed away last year before Thanksgiving with a heart attack. He left his will with instructions not to open it nor to contact you until six months had passed. In his will, he left you and your children a considerable amount of money with instructions that I personally deliver the check to you. He only asked that you live happily and if at all possible, keep the farm in the family.   You are to receive a stated amount each year until it is used up and this is the first check."

Handing the envelope and copy of the will to Elroy, he further stated, "If you have any questions concerning the will, you have been instructed to contact me or one of my partners at this address. Oh yes, one other thing. He requests that your children receive a college education and he has made financial arrangements for that to be done. Is there anything else I can help you with?"

Too stunned to answer, Judy broke down and cried. Elroy tried to comfort her but it was no use. She ran into the house, hugged the children, and then went to the bedroom.

Elroy thanked Mr. Cookhouse, told him he didn't know what to say, thanked him again and invited him to stay for supper.

"I just believe I will, Mr. Masterson. I was told by Win that your wife was the best cook he had ever been fortunate enough to dine with."

Mr. Cookhouse left immediately after supper, wanting to get back to Ohio before it was too dark. "These roads you have here aren't the best, Elroy, if I may call you that."

They could not convince him to stay overnight so waving goodbye, they walked up on the porch, still stunned by their loss of Win, and now having more money than they thought possible.

*****

Twenty years later, Elroy and Judy proudly sat and watched Lonnie receive his college degree and he was going to go on and attend medical school. Elsie had graduated the year before, became a teacher, and had married her childhood sweetheart.

*****

Driving up the now paved, twisting narrow road, they stopped as their house came into sight around a bend. They parked the car beside the road, walked arm in arm to the house, and listened to the wind as it moved gently over the hills.

They would live out their lives in the little farmhouse. The children came as often as possible and the grandchildren spent the summers with them; working, playing, laughing, and enjoying the beauty of childhood. It was an era of peace up there on the Creek. The winds carried Win's spirit over the hills and down into the valley and covered them all with LOVE.

MAUDIE

Maudie pulled her bonnet down over her head to try and keep the searing July sun off her face and neck. She was light skinned and learned long ago that it didn't pay for her to expose herself to the sun for long. Barefooted, she walked out past the well, up the little ridge, to the outhouse. Noticing that there were very few Sears Roebuck pages left, she made a mental note to bring out the latest copy which she had just received. The pictures in the book were pretty but she could only wish for things. Maudie and Everett were dirt poor. They lived mostly off the garden out back and the few hogs they could raise for meat although they did have chickens for meat and eggs. Once a month the government truck from Grayson came up on the Creek with butter, some lard, sugar, and mostly things the folks couldn't raise. Times were hard there in the valley in the year nineteen hundred seventeen and the folks worked together to try and make it easier for all of them. Today Maudie was going up to the schoolhouse to collect her rations doled out by the government and Everett was going to start a hole for a new outhouse. When he finished with that, he was going to Buffalo Creek to hunt for turtles.

Walking up the road, with an occasional side trip to the few remaining creek pools to cool her feet, Maudie felt like she owned the world. Never having been away from home, never really knowing what was out there, she felt good about her life and the years she had spent with Everett. They had no children but had some nieces and nephews, most of whom had left the valley for distant parts. Sometimes they would get a letter but usually nothing was heard from the ones who had gone away. Maudie's sister, Fern, had often said that her two children were too ashamed of the folks on the Creek to ever return.

On this hot July day, Maudie had no cares. She had eggs and biscuits for breakfast, had fed Everett a good meal, and now she was on the way to get some more supplies, mainly flour and sugar. She had plenty of lard and got her butter from Fern, who had a few milk cows on her farm. Oh, she had looked over the Sears Roebuck catalog but that was another world to her and she really didn't feel any desire to be a part of that world. To Fern, she would say, "Those dresses sure look pretty, don't they? But where would we wear them if we had them?"

Stopping along the road to check on some ripening blackberries and making a mental note to come soon to pick them, she heard a wagon coming up the road. There were the Smiths from over on the other side of the hills coming to get their rations. Waving at them, she turned down an offer to ride, "Lordy, I can't stand that woman," came quietly from her mouth.

"We'll meet you at the school, Maudie, and you can ride back home with us." Mrs. Smith waved back.

In a little cloud of dust, the wagon pulled away from Maudie as she pulled some ripe berries from the nearby bushes. Singing a little ditty she had learned from her ma, she went on her way, not hurrying, but enjoying all that the creek had to offer. It was almost dry and some of the farmers were worrying about where to get water for their cattle and hogs. Usually the creek ran dry most of July and August and every year that Maudie could remember, the farmers worried about water for their livestock. Wells were hard to dig in the rock beneath the surface but most people had them and always carried enough water to the animals for them to get by.

Maudie and Everett had grown up together, played together as youngsters, helped their parents out on the farm, and eventually, while in school, they began to get a little more serious. It was taken for granted there on the Creek, that the youngsters would get married at an early age. Some of the families had land to pass on to their children, some had nothing, but that didn't keep the young people from getting married. Those that didn't usually left the creek and never returned. Maudie was just sixteen and Everett was seventeen when the visiting preacher came to visit on a hot Sunday in August, in the year nineteen hundred two. It was too hot to go into the building for services so the people sat around a large sycamore tree and used what shade they could as they listened to a sermon by the preacher. Finally, one of the women stood up and said she had to get home to fix her granny's meal, and that pretty much ended the service. Later that day, the preacher visited with Everett's folks and Maudie happened to be there with her ma and pa. Everett simply said, "Maudie, let's you and me get hitched?"

"Everett, don't you think we ought to talk about it first? I'm willing but this may be a little sudden."

With the parents of both of them listening, Everett spoke up. "Now Maudie, you know we want a church wedding but the preacher won't be back this way until fall. It's too hot in the church so let's me and you have him marry us right here. Whatcha' say?"

Looking at her ma and pa, and seeing no objection from them, she said, "All right Everett, let's do it."

*****

Maudie walked along, keeping in the shade of the overhanging tree branches as much as possible and thought of the past married years of her life. "I'm thirty years old and I've had me a good life with Everett. One of these days, we're going to have us a baby. I just know we are!"

Passing by Everett's brother's house, Maudie waved to Watt, and when Cindy, Watt's wife, asked her in to rest a spell, she gladly walked over to the porch, got a cool drink from the water jug, and joined Cindy and Watt on the steps.

"Sure is a hot one, Cindy. I've been walking along the creek bed but there isn't much water to wade in. There was a little pool down by Omer's place and I sat there and cooled my feet for a little while. Are you going up to the school? I need me some flour and sugar but that's about all I'll get this time. They tell me that the government is getting tired of bringing us food every month, what with the war and all. Don't know what we'll do if they stop coming. I don't understand this thing they call politics. I know that a man came around last week and asked Everett to vote for him. Said he might be able to help us out a little if he was elected."

"I betcha' that was the same man who came by here asking for our vote. He seemed a little funny to me. I told Watt we shouldn't vote for him unless he offered us some money.   I think all he wanted to give us was some 'shine and since we don't drink, he left in a hurry. " Cindy laughed at that. "Betcha' he will get the Smith's vote!"

"I don't doubt that a bit." Maudie laughed with her. "They offered to give me a ride to the school house but I turned them down. That Flossie Smith, if she don't beat all. Pretending to be a bit better than we are and here she is, going to get food like the rest of us."

Watt called out to his daughter, "Hey Dody!"

"Whatcha' want, Pa?"

"I wantcha' to go down to the melon patch and get a good ripe'un and put it in the creek to cool. We have company here. You come and say howdy to Maudie."

Dody, coming to the porch, "Cain't Pauly get the melon, Pa? I'm busy right now fixin' my hair. Howdy, Aunt Maudie."

"Dody, you know if Paul goes he will bring back a small one and we need a big one. You go on now. Get it and then you can fix your hair. That boy won't notice no how. He only has eyes for food and you cain't see that yet."

"Awright, Pa. I'm agoin' but Pauly can help, cain't he?"

"I reckon he can. Paul, you go on with your sister and help her with the melon."

"Papa, she'll just try and get me to carry it. I might drop it and you would give me a whoppin' fer shore. Tell her not to make me carry it."

"Now listen here, you two. I'm going to take a willow switch to both of you iffn' you don't do what I say. I don't care how old you are. Now go on and do as I say. Hey Dody, you carry that melon and don't drop it. And hurry it up. It needs time to cool down. I'll tell the boy friend you can't see him tonight!"

Laughing as he watched his two children walk slowly down the dirt lane, he called out to them, "And make sure it's ripe!"

Dody was developing into a beautiful girl and would soon be sixteen years old. She was almost ready to go away to high school, a little older than most beginning high schoolers, but she had been out of school for two years so she could help around the house after her mother had died. Ginny had died suddenly, maybe for lack of medical attention, but most likely from overwork on the farm. She had been a strong woman and had helped Watt do most everything including plowing and woodcutting. In spite of him telling her to let him do the work, she had insisted that she help out. He remembered what had happened just a few days before her death.

"Watt, you go on to Carter to get our supplies and I promise not to do any more wood chopping. Go on with you now. I'm going to be fine."

When Watt came back from the store, he found her out in the field plowing behind the two old mules. Running to her, he called, "Ginny, you get yourself up here right now. You told me you wouldn't do any work today."

"Watt, I only told you I wouldn't chop any wood. This field needs plowing and I thought I would help you out. All right, I'll quit. But you put the mules in the field and come on up to the house. I need some wood for the cook stove before I can cook supper. And I'm going to make you some of your favorite food, wilted lettuce and sweet potatoes."

"That's enough to make me do as you say. I'll be right there."

When Watt got up to the house, he found Ginny bent over the porch railing vomiting up blood. He took her by her arm and carefully walked her into the bedroom where he placed her on the bed and went to get a pan and some cool water from the well.

Wiping off the sweat on her forehead, he talked soothingly to her and explained that she must take it easy.

"Ginny, I'm going to hitch up the wagon tomorrow and take you to the doctor in Grayson. We have to do something about you working all the time."

Calling out to Dody as he heard her come into the house, "Hey Dody, your ma's bad sick and I need you to go up to get Mrs. Walker to come help. Go on now and hurry. Tell Paul to feed the hogs and gather the eggs. Hurry, honey."

"Pa, cain't I help?"

"Go on, Dody, do as I say. When you get back you can help, but we need Mrs. Walker."

Yelling out to Paul to do what pa had said, she began to run up the road to the Walker's. It was maybe a mile but she ran most of the way. Panting, she called to Mrs. Walker, from the front porch.

"Pa says momma is bad sick and he needs you. Can you come now?"

"Sure I can, Dody." Calling to her husband, Bill, she told him to hook up the buggy in a hurry because she had to go to Watt's to help Ginny.

As they climbed into the buggy, Peggy asked Dody what the trouble seemed to be.

"I don't rightly know, Mrs. Walker. Pa just told me to come get you as fast as I could and I did. That's all I know."

Keeping the horse at a trot, they soon arrived and Mrs. Walker ran in the front door and called out to Watt.

He answered her from the bedroom and as soon as she saw Ginny, Peggy realized that there was trouble ahead.

"Dody, you go get me some cold water, and Watt, you get some towels so I can wipe her off and cool her down. She's running a terrible fever."

"I need to take her to the doctor in Grayson as soon as she is able to travel in the wagon."

"Watt, she won't be able to make the trip until the fever goes down so I'll stay here and care for her. Would you mind going to tell Bill to come down as soon as he can and he can bring me some things I'll need?"

"I'll go right now and take Paul with me. I don't want him to see his ma looking like this. Hey Dody, I'm going to go to the Walker's with Paul and we won't be gone long. You help Peggy with whatever she needs." Dody had been standing on the porch waiting for someone to tell her how her ma was feeling. Paul, a nice looking boy of thirteen had come up to her and tears were in his eyes.

"Is ma all right, Dody? Can I go see her?"

Pa wants you to go to the Walker's with him. Why don't you go to the barn and hook up the horse to our buggy so you can take it instead of the Walker's? Ma'll be all right. She just needs to rest. We'll have to help with the chores. You help Pa and I'll do the housework. I'll even cook for you!"

"Ugh!" Paul replied as he ran off to the barn.

Ginny kept getting worse and two days later she died.

*****

Watt had known Cindy for years and she was now a widow and a woman was needed around the house so he asked Cindy to marry him and she agreed. It was maybe a little soon after Ginny's death for them to marry, but Watt felt he needed help with the children and he and Cindy talked it over and decided to go ahead.

Cindy had come to the Creek as a young bride from North Carolina. Old man Stewart had brought her back as the wife of his young son, Dale. Stewart had worked for a man in North Carolina as a tobacco grader and had seen Cindy working in the fields and bought her for his son. She was part Cherokee and had very little say in what happened to her. The owner of the tobacco fields was only too glad to get rid of her since she was complaining to the authorities and eventually they would catch up with the man.

*****

Maudie and Cindy had become good friends and often visited with each other. Maudie kept insisting that she had to go so Cindy said, "Now, Maudie, you know Watt has sent for a watermelon for us and I insist you stop by here on your way home and we will have a cool melon to eat. Maybe I can get Watt to go down and get Everett while you're gone and we can visit a bit.

Maudie left to go get her sugar and flour and giving in to her being tired, accepted a ride with the Smith's back to Watt's house. The Smith's lingered a bit at Watt's, hoping they would get invited to come in and share some melon, but when they weren't asked , they drove off.

Watt and Everett arrived shortly after Maudie.

"What was wrong with the Smith's? They hardly spoke as they passed us. You say something to them, Maudie?"

"No, I didn't! They wanted us to ask them in for some melon but when Cindy didn't, they drove off."

Watt and Everett walked down to the creek to get the melon.

"Hey, Dody! You and Paul come on and have a piece of melon with us."

"Pa, I have to get ready to go. Donny is going to take me to Grayson and it is getting late. Pauly went up the road so he isn't here. You go ahead and I'll be there as soon as I can."

Sitting there in the shade of the porch, they enjoyed the pieces of watermelon and soon a buggy pulled into the yard of the house, and a young man got out.

"Dody will be down in a minute, Donny. Come on over and have a piece of melon. You know Maudie and Everett, don't you?"

"Yes sir, Mr. Watt. I surely do. Howdy, Everett. Howdy, Maudie. Sure is a hot one."

Dody came down the stairs and asked Donny to help her with her things and while he was bringing her bags to the buggy, she said goodbye to Maudie and Everett. The she hugged her pa and Cindy and promised to write often and come home as much as she could.

Even though she was only the stepmother, Cindy had grown to like Dody and Paul very much. "Now don't you two youngn's get in any trouble. Dody, you study hard and come on back home as much as you can."

Watt tried to hold back tears but they were there, rolling down his cheeks as he walked Dody to the buggy, and gave her a kiss. "I love you, little girl. Don't you forget that, and don't you ever forget your ma."

"I won't, Pa. I surely won't." Paul came to the house as they were leaving and Donny stopped the buggy so they could say goodbye.

Hugging Paul, they turned and waved goodbye and rode off.

*****

Dody had gone off to school, eventually married Donny and they moved out to Oregon where Donny had taken a job in a large lumber mill. She had come home one time before they moved, and when she left, she made Watt and Cindy promise to come visit them. They agreed to go when she and Donny got settled and soon after Dody left, Paul joined them out West.

About a year later, Dody wrote them that Donny had a good job and they wanted Watt and Cindy to come see them. She sent them money for train tickets and arrangements were made for Everett and Maudie to care for the farm while they were gone.

Watt said they would only be gone for a few months but after a month had passed, he wrote Everett that they had decided to stay with Dody and Donny and he was giving the farm to Everett. He wrote, "Someday, Brother, I'll come back to see you but the farm is all yours and all I ask is that you let us come visit."

Being the oldest brother, Watt had inherited the main farm from his father and Everett had been given a tract of land down near the mouth of the creek. The land was not good for farming so Everett never did much with it.

Watt, in his letter, had asked for Everett to send him a few of his belongings.

"There are some things pa gave me up in the attic which I would like to have. Go look in the old trunk and send me the things in it. Cindy has some things in a box up there which she would like to have. We don't want any of the clothes or the furniture. There is an old iron table with a glass top which has been passed down through the family, you know which one I'm talking about. I'd like for you to keep that but do what you want with the rest."

*****

Two old men were sitting on the porch swing and a woman was sitting on the steps shelling peas as the car rolled up the dirt road and stopped in front of the house. It was early spring of the year nineteen hundred fifty.

A young woman got out of the car and walked over to the porch. "Excuse me folks, I'm looking for a Mrs. McGlone. I was told at the grocery store in Carter that she lived around here and they gave me directions. Am I at the right place?"

Grabbing her cane, Cindy got up from the steps, walked over to the car, and said to the lady, "I reckon I'm the only Mrs.

166

McGlone here right now. Everett's wife, Maudie, is down to the barn if she's the one you want to see. Everett and Maudie live here.   And you call me Cindy for sure." Chuckling to herself, "And who might you be, young lady? And that's a fine looking automobile you have there."

My name is Orene McGlone and I'm looking for some of my folks who I'm told, lived here or near here at one time. I don't know which Mrs. McGlone I'm looking for. I was just given the name of Mrs. McGlone to talk to."

"My sakes now! So you're a McGlone? Honey, the McGlones still live here. We live most all over the Creek. Why don't you come up here and sit with me on the steps and you can help shell peas while we talk---if you know how to, that is!"

Taking her pan of peas off the porch banister, and sitting it on her apron, Cindy offered some of the peas to Orene.

"Now tell us which of the McGlones are your kin."

Sitting down by Cindy, Orene said her father was Theodore McGlone and his father was Ernest McGlone. "I don't know any more than that, I'm afraid."

Maudie came up from the barn and the five of them sat and talked a long time.   Maudie said she thought Ernest was Ezekiel's boy so that would make Orene a distant relative.

Evening shadows began to creep across the tiny hills of the valley and the smell of fresh blooming lilac began to sweep across on the softly blowing wind.

Watt told Orene how the McGlones had come to settle on the Creek. "Our great grandfather had settled here with his wife and they had two children, three really, one had died in infancy. Jim was the oldest. Everett and I came from Jim's family line. I have two children, Dody and Paul. They live out in Oregon and that's where we live now. We're back to visit a spell."

Maudie brought out some cookies and invited Orene to stay the night. Orene looked to be in her early twenties and said she was not married-yet! Laughing when Watt questioned her, "It may change real soon though."

"My grandfather was born in the early nineteen hundreds and served in the big War.   He loved this valley and when he came back from the War, he met Grandmother Ida, and they got married about nineteen twenty.

Watt, after telling Orene to be sure and call him Watt instead of Mr. McGlone, said he was going to turn in. "We'll talk more in the morning, Orene."

Saying good night to Maudie and Everett, he said he would see them for breakfast and they could all talk.

Cindy stayed up a little longer and they all watched the stars come out in the darkening night. Easter was a few days away and Orene agreed to stay until the day after but she then had to get home to work.

"We're going to have an Easter egg hunt at the church and would love to have you stay and join in the fun. You can help me dye the eggs and we'll do that after breakfast tomorrow." Maudie and Orene took an immediate liking to each other and going inside, spent most of the evening sitting by the fireside talking about the 'outside' world, a world that Maudie had seldom experienced.

"You can see, Orene, that we have few modern facilities except for electricity. I doubt if we will ever have water other than well water. I've only been out of the County twice, no, three times, and I just am amazed at what I saw there. I think telephones were the greatest things I saw but running water was also something to see. We went once to see our son, Eddie, but he went away to the army last year and we haven't heard from him since. It's so unlike him not to keep in touch with us."

Interrupting, Orene said she might be able to check on him when she got back home to Ohio. "I'll see what I can find out. I work out at an airbase there and maybe I can get someone to help me find him."

"That would be wonderful! We think something has happened to him but don't know who to call."

Hearing the old clock ring out the hour, Maudie said, "I think we had best get to bed. I have some chores to do tomorrow and I imagine Everett and Watt will want to visit with you some. You sleep as long as you like. I'll get some water for you to wash with and you can use the lantern to go to the outhouse. Maybe I'd better show you where it is. It gets dark around here and sometimes it is hard to stay on the path."

The next day was born nice and sunny with the promise of a beautiful day. Orene woke and looked around her at the sparse furniture and for a moment, wondered how anyone could live like this and be happy. Then, as though someone spoke to her, she thought of the good clean life they lived here in the valley, and yes, the times were hard on the people but they were not burdened down with the stress of outside worldly living. Washing her face, she looked at her watch and found she had slept most of the morning.

"Well now, Miss Orene, do we serve you breakfast or lunch?" Maudie wiped her hands on her apron, laughed with Orene, and gave her a hug. "We're so glad you came to see us. We seldom have company and you are something special. Watt and Everett are eagerly awaiting your time with them and have promised to show you around the valley, by Everett's buggy! He said that fancy automobile won't go where they are going to take you."

On the way back to the kitchen from the outhouse, Orene stopped to look at the old well with boards around it's sides to keep anything from falling in. The bucket hanging there had been used and some water was dripping from it back into the well. Thinking to herself, I don't believe that is very safe drinking water, but no one here seems to get sick drinking it so I suppose it is all right."

Washing her hands and eating a big breakfast of ham, eggs, and grits, Orene was interrupted by Everett coming in the door. "Girl, I've got almost a full day's chores done and have been waiting for you for hours. Guess we're going to have to teach you country living. Come on now, I have the horse and buggy waiting for us. Have you ever ridden in a buggy?"

Taking Everett by the hand, "No sir, I don't believe I have but I can't think of a better time than right now to learn and I can't think of a better person to teach me."

With little dust swirls playing around the horse's hooves and Everett driving, they settled in to a slow pace as Watt told her about the valley as the three moved up the dirt road. Sometimes they had to use the creek bed for a road but the water was not deep enough to bother them.

They rode by the old log cabin where the old men, Watt and Everett had first lived. Then they stopped at the one room school/church house and Watt told her he had built for the folks of the community to come to learn and to worship. Going on up the road, they passed the cemetery on the hill and then Watt stopped at an old deserted house and said to Orene, "I want to tell you a story about a special person in the valley. She lived in this house until she married many years ago and moved far away. She convinced me and her ma to come live with them and this is our first trip back to the Creek since we left many years ago. She was special because everyone up here loved her; she was beautiful, and she was my daughter. She used to play in that little pool of water right over there. She and her brother, Paul, would catch crawdads and watch the dragonflies flit around them. The tale was that there were snakes around when the dragonflies were near. Then there were the little turtles she and Paul caught and would sometimes bring them home where her ma, Ginny, put them in a barrel and said she would fatten them up and have some good turtle meat for supper one day soon."

They drove up one of the little branches until they came to an old, rotted out frame house.

"If you are from Ezekiel's branch, this is where he lived and I expect Ernest, was born here. Ezekiel and his wife had eleven children but they all left as they got of age."

Everett stopped the buggy so Orene could get out and look around. The old house still had some newspaper lining the walls and Everett told her that was to help keep out the cold winds. She took a few pictures and as Watt walked over to the creek bank he called for Orene to come see.

"Lookey there. Now that's a nice looking snake if I ever saw one."

Orene looked down and on the edge of the water, was a long black snake and she recoiled in horror.

"Aw, that thing won't hurt you, Missy. I didn't mean to scare you."

Everett had picked it up to show Orene that it wouldn't hurt. Watt laughed as she pulled away.

Going back to the buggy, Watt started to tell Orene about Dody. "Everett's daughter is named after my Dody, only it's Dotty, not Dody. And she's a pretty one too, almost as pretty as the original."

"Go ahead with your story, Watt. I really want to hear it."

"Well, one Sunday morning we were having church services and the preacher was really into his sermon when all of a sudden, he stopped, stared at the back door as it opened, and there stood a tiny little girl, all dirty, only partly clothed, and crying. She may have been four or five, but we never found out. Ginny stood up, walked back to the little girl, wrapped her in her arms and walked out the door. The preacher said he would finish the sermon on the next Sunday he could make it here. You see, he was a preacher who went to different churches and maybe he wouldn't be back here for several weeks. He had a prayer, asked Brother Walker to serve communion, and then dismissed the people. Walking outside, there was no sign of Ginny or the little girl. People visited for awhile and then slowly left for their homes."

Maudie had come up the road to tell Watt that Ginny had taken the little girl home with her and was going to clean her up.

"We kept that little girl, named her Dody, and later Ginny gave me a son, Paul. Everett, here, had two children but they were born after we left for Oregon.

We've seen enough for today and me and Everett have to tend to the chores. Let's go back and we'll do some more exploring tomorrow."

That afternoon Watt and Everett sat on the porch looking out over the farm where they had grown up. Watt had become somewhat of a land baron in Oregon but now he and Cindy had returned to the creek so they could visit once again with Everett and Maudie. Rocking back and forth in the rocker just about asleep, Everett didn't hear Cindy and Maudie and Orene drive up in Orene's car.

Walking up the steps, Maudie walked over to Everett, said hello, and startled, Everett stood up and gave her a hug. "I guess I must have been lost in thought. I didn't even hear you come in. Where's Watt?"

"He, Cindy and Orene have just gone down to the barn to look at the new pigs."

The three came back to the house and Watt and Cindy said they were going to take a walk down by the creek. They changed clothes and they walked off hand in hand to follow a pathway of many years ago, if it was still there.

Everett, coming out on the front lawn, watched them go. He and Maudie had enjoyed the visit with Watt and Cindy and as they disappeared down behind the brush, he said to Orene, "You know it's going to be hard for me to see them leave. I know we'll never see each other again. And me and Watt had so much fun here while we grew up. We never had anything. Me and Maudie were poor as poor could be but when Watt decided to stay out West, he gave this place to us. Watt wants us to go west with them, but I don't want to sell this place. I suppose he's right when he says I've earned a rest from farming but I have mixed emotions about leaving. Maybe I can talk him into staying here!"

*****

Watt and Cindy walked along the now brush overgrown creek bank until they came to what he thought was the little stream coming down from the hillside. Following it to the tree covered spot, he found it to be about the same as when he left it. The little dam he had built was now gone and the water was only a trickle but the soft cool moss was still there and he and Cindy sat down and quietly watched the afternoon move on.

Finally, Cindy spoke and began to recall the day of their wedding.

*****

Riding along, Watt had whispered to Cindy, "We're not going to have much privacy on our one night honeymoon. Why don't we take some blankets and camp out at a spot I know real well? We won't get much rest if we stay at Charlie's place."

"Watt! Why do you want to get me alone? And what makes you think you're going to get any sleep anyway?" Laughing, they arrived at the church. "Watt, does anyone else know of that place?"

As Watt got out of the buggy, Brother Everett came up to meet him and carried him in his arms to the building. "This is so you won't get cold feet and run out on Cindy." Watt laughed as they put him down inside the building.

Cindy was a beautiful woman. Her hair was dark; some said the color of a raven. She had deep-set ebony eyes, eyes that could burn a hole in your soul. When she looked at Watt with love in those eyes, he just seemed to melt. And on this day, there was nothing but love about this beautiful copper colored part Cherokee maiden.

Everett and Watt stood up as the preacher approached. The preacher wiped his brow, "Ladies and gentlemen, we are ready for this blessed event to begin. Watt, you and Everett come this way."

After the wedding, Watt and Cindy went back to the house to change clothes. They decided to leave before anyone came home. Walking down by the creek, they came upon the turn-off to Watt's 'hideaway' and turning into the meadow, they soon came to the spot. Cindy saw the clear but shallow pool, and laughing, said, "Watt, I'm going to take a bath in that cool water." While bathing, things developed into a little more than talking! They found the mossy spot, wrapped themselves in each other's arms, and Cindy, so still, so delightful, so much like a fresh flower with its bloom ready to burst open, kissed Watt longingly and deeply. Her long legs stretched out and Watt reached to touch her with his finger, moving ever so slowly, so gently, not to hurt her but to tell her of his dreams. She turned to him and her canyon dark eyes opened to gaze at him. She smiled, Watt reached out to her, to feel her warmth, to say to her words that were so lacking but so full of meaning.

Watt had spread out the blankets and just as darkness settled in, Cindy said, "Watt, you keep your hands to yourself. What do you think I am? Here I gave you a blanket to keep you warm and you're trying to take advantage of me! I want you to know, sir, that I am a proper married woman!"

"Yes ma'am, I do know you are. I asked your husband if I could hold you up close to me and he said it would be all right with him. They laughed together and then all was quiet, as Cindy liked to hear the night noises of the crickets and the frogs. Once she heard the singing of a whippoorwill and life, as it started off for the two of them, was good.

The night shadows had been blown away by the wind and the morning star came out to greet them and to shine upon this beautiful forest nymph, this woman who glowed like a newly opened rose bud, fresh, filled with love which made her eyes sparkle as diamonds of dew in the morning mist. She was as beautiful as the butterfly; she was as lovely as the sunbeam that stole into the shadows to send its light.

As she awakened to the new day, a tiny beam of sunlight penetrated the deep, dark forest, and out of the morning mist of time, she rose from the dew covered bed of moss, stretched her body, and smiled at Watt, the smile of eternal love. The shadowed creek down below them, wound its way along the tree lined banks, and sparkling drops of water, like tiny diamonds, dropped from her body, as she washed away the sleep of the night. Her body, as free as the morning winds...

Singing to herself, Cindy walked along the stream bed chewing on a blade of fresh grass, watching the clouds move slowly in the deep blue sky. She removed her shoes, tiptoed to the edge of the water eddy, and let the cool water run over her ankles. A blue jay greeted the morning by chatting noisily in a nearby beach tree, telling her not to disturb it anymore. Laughing at the bird's antics, she moved to the moss bed of the night before, removed her dress, lay down on the soft bed up close to the sleeping Watt, and stretched her body to let the sunlight reach her already brown body.

The quietness of the morning, along with the warmth of the sun, made her drowsy again and soon she was off to a land of dreams.

An eye opened! Someone had placed a blanket beside her. Jumping up while wrapping her dress about her, she smiled when she saw Watt grinning at her. He grabbed her and pulled her down beside him.

"Now I know why you wanted to come out here in this place. You didn't want to just show me the place. You wanted to get me out here in the bushes all alone. And, my good man, what are your intentions this morning? I told you before, I'm a proper married woman!"

"And I told you before, I have your husband's permission to lie here on this blanket with you."

"But I think you have more on your mind than that!"

"And what's wrong with that, young lady?"

"Nothing! Nothing at all! Just keep on wanting me." She moved to him as he held out his arms.

*****

They walked again through the meadow and headed for Charlie's house, Watt's cousin. They watched as the great ball in the sky disappeared among some clouds as though some monstrous fish ate it. As the rays disappeared, thunder began to roll across the valley and lightning streaked in its glory as the clouds now created a semi-darkness over the entire land.

The rain began as the thunder now became deeper and lightning flashed closer. A hasty retreat to a nearby cliff gave them some shelter but the summer wind saw to it that even a cliff could not hide them from the whims of Nature's storms. Sheets of water raced down the creek blocking their view from the nearby hill. The freshness of the land permeated the air. The sounds of the storm slowly disappeared over the hills and the same warm rays of the late afternoon sun came back to dry them and the clouds turned soft and white and puffy looking. A robin landed near them and pulled a worm from the earth, a squirrel quarreled at them for being too close, and a cow gave out a long lonely moo from somewhere on top the ridge.

As suddenly as it appeared, the storm moved on. It became eerily quiet. Then a tiny light permeated the cave where Watt and Cindy had taken shelter, just a tiny beam in the darkness of the cave. They returned to their moss covered spot, found it to be rather wet, but they had kept the blanket they had carried from the house, with them and it was dry. Now night was approaching and they both decided they wanted to stay here for another night rather than at Charlie's. Eating the two sandwiches they had made before leaving the house, they lay there on the blanket, each with their own thoughts and finally darkness settled in. They looked over the nearby hillside and saw the giant full moon start its rise above the distant horizon. It filled the earth with the radiance of its glory and drove away the darkness of the night. Shortly the quietness was disturbed as the sounds of the night creatures began. The sound of a barking dog could be heard, and then another, and then the night was a chorus of animal sounds.

A leg moved, long and beautiful. His hand traced its outline as a sigh came from her heart. A tiny breeze played against the tree leaves and a tiny finger of light came from the moon as the curtain was briefly blown aside. The moonlight crossed over her body and filled the dark area with the tiniest of light. Like a soft breeze, Watt had come to the blanket and her arms reached out like tentacles for him. The wind seemed to whisper to him....come, come to me my love, let me be your heart, your soul. Come... come----

Watt lay beside Cindy, his lips reached out to find her as the moonlight and breeze played over their blanket covering. They heard not a sound except the beating of two hearts as one.

Watt touched her, slowly moving his fingers over the mounds of her beauty, reaching with his lips to taste her sweetness. A tiny breath blown into his ear, a caress across her brow, the seal of his lips on her eyes. Slowly he moved beside her with his tongue darting to and fro on her body, reaching for her nipples to feel them hardening at his touch, feeling around her shoulder with the velvety touch of dancing fingers.

She stretched to let the moonbeam cover her body, and there in its light, the beauty of this Cherokee angel was exposed, exposed in all its glory for him to see. Great sighs of love came from his heart and his soul reached for words to express this love as they moved together, slowly at first, and then as the light of the moon disappeared, a storm raged within them, and a voiced softly called out... Yes! Yes! Love me! Love me!"

Bells rang out and the great ringing sound of them echoed in their ears as the fulfillment of their bodies joined as one. Rivers of moisture rolled from their bodies as the stillness of the night returned, broken only by loud breathing, by the feel of love, and the light of the moon again shone through the opening, and in the trees, the night wind sighed as it gently raced across the Creek.

Cindy lay there on the moss, body outstretched, and she lay with the knowledge that forever, she would be a loving memory to Watt. She would know in her dreams of her man, who loved her beyond knowledge. Then she heard him as he gently turned over to sleep, "Rest well, my Cindy Moon, my Cherokee maiden."

Now, these many years later, she sat there on the moss, reached for his hand, and told him she loved him so much!

Back at the house, Everett and Maudie had completed the day's chores and were sitting on the front porch in the swing. They had said good bye to Orene and told her they would write to her and asked her to come see them again if they still lived here. One of the neighbors had come by and Everett had told him he might sell the farm and move to the West to be near Watt and Cindy.

"There's nothing to keep us here, John. We have no family, I'm getting too old to farm, and besides, I want to see some of the country. Oh, I'll miss the farm. That's for sure! But someday I may come back to see it just like Watt has finally come back this time. John, you and the missus be sure to come see us before we leave."

Everett had a buyer in mind for the farm but had not signed any papers. They began to pack up what they wanted to take with them. The attic was the hardest part to clean out. There were lots of memories up there and Everett and Watt had a few choked emotions as they went through the trunks and boxes. Finally a decision was made to take only three trunks with them and to burn the rest.

It was mid-August when Everett was ready to move out. Watt had stayed to help and the trunks would be shipped by train to their new home and Everett and Maudie would go with Watt and Cindy. Their belongings would be taken to Olive Hill by truck where they would be loaded on the train for the journey west.

They were to leave Sunday morning after church and on Saturday night, the folks of the Creek were going to hold a farewell party for them.

Maudie came to Everett before the party, crying. "Do we have to go, Everett? I know we can't do the farm work anymore but we can sell the land and keep the house. I remember when I was a young woman, I would walk up here barefooted with my bonnet and apron on, to get food from the government. Those were happy days, even if we had nothing. Now, the Lord has given us so much and this is our home. Oh, never mind. You know I love you and I'll go wherever you want to go."

Everett jumped up from the rocker and said, "Maudie, I was only doing it for you. I don't want to go either. We'll stay." Both crying, they told Watt and Cindy they couldn't leave, and when they went to the party, Everett told the people of their decision, but they would have the party for Watt and Cindy.

Next morning, Everett and Watt said goodbye. Knowing this would be the last time they would see each other, they parted as the mid-August sun beat down on them. Maudie and Cindy hugged and promised to write.

Watt slowly drove around the nearby bend in the road, stopped his rented car, got out, waved one final goodbye to Everett, then he and Cindy continued back to their home in the West.

Everett and Maudie remained living in their valley home for the rest of their days, content in the knowledge that the choice had been theirs.

I'M GOING HOME

Ernie parked his car and rushed to the apartment to see his grandmother who was standing in her front window waving to him.

Grandma and Grandpa McCarty had always been favorites of Ernie and he regretted that his work now kept him from seeing them as often as he would like. It had been two years since Ernie had been home and although he had seen his parents when they visited him, he had not seen his grandparents since he left for Hawaii.

"Grandma, you look the same as you did when I left, maybe even prettier! I've certainly missed seeing you."

Hugging her tightly, he told her to wipe away the tears.

"I'm going to be here for a few days and we don't need tears. I want to see that big smile you always had for me. Come on! Let's go down to the drug store and have a soda."

When he was growing up, he and his grandma would often walk to the drug store where she would order him a pineapple soda and they would sit there and listen to the jukebox music.

"I guess I grew up on pineapple sodas, Grandma. But they were never as good as your cooking was."

"Now, Ernie. You know you don't want to go anywhere while I have this fresh blackberry jam cake just out of the oven. Or, maybe you don't remember my blackberry cakes and will want me to send this to your brother?"

She took Ernie, now a man of thirty five, by the hand, led him to the kitchen and showed him the tantalizing cake with the powered sugar icing sitting on the counter.

"I remember when you made the first one for me, Grandma. Dad always expected one for Christmas and when I got a 'little' taste of his, I asked you to make one just for me alone. And you did! What was I? About eight years old I think. Have you missed a year since I was eight? Oh yes, you did miss last year because I was so far away you couldn't get it to me and that was the time grandpa had to leave."

Suddenly, quietness settled over the kitchen.

"How is he? From what I heard from dad, it's pretty bad. You know, I want to see him for myself. Dad said it would be of no use, that he wouldn't know me, but I have to go. I need to see him one more time, although I'll admit, something inside me tells me I really don't want to. I'd like to remember him like he was but I know he's getting old and this disease is a horrible thing. I'd like to have you go with me, but I would also like to see him alone, to remember how he used to be. I hope you understand. Dad didn't seem to think it would be a good idea for me to go alone."

"Ernie, you go on and see him. No, he won't know you nor does he know anyone else. He hasn't shown any recognition of me for several months now. I think I told you on the phone that he's suffering quietly, but I somehow doubt if he feels anything, either physically or mentally. It was hard for me to put him in the nursing home but it had to be. I had several small strokes trying to take care of him and finally my doctor told me there was no other choice. Your dad has taken good care of him and goes to see him at least every other day."

She held onto Ernie's hand as he prepared to leave.

"You do what you think is best. It won't be pleasant seeing him like he is now, but go on if you feel you need to. I'll talk with your dad and we'll go over to see him tomorrow."

Ernie hugged his grandmother again and left. He turned and waved at her as he got into his car and he could see her wiping away a tear. He loved his grandma and memories came back to him as he drove to the nursing home. Many times she had taken care of him when he was little and always had cooked up a special meal whenever he asked her. He had spent almost every summer with her while he was growing up. She had taken him on his first train ride, grandpa had taken him fishing, and they were always there when he needed advice. Laughingly, he said to himself, "I didn't always follow it, however!"

Pulling into the parking lot of the nursing home, he again paused and gave serious thought about going inside.

"If I don't go see him, then I can always remember how he was before. But, if I don't go in, can I ever forgive myself for not doing so? Maybe I'll just look in on him and leave."

Entering the front door, he approached the nursing station to ask for directions to the room. The nurse on duty told him she would show him the way and as they walked down the aisle, Ernie told her who he was and how much he loved his grandpa.

"Sir, I'm afraid you'll be shocked when you see him. Prepare yourself to see a 'stranger,' and understand, he's not suffering. Your dad and grandmother leave here quite often in tears and sometimes I wonder if it would be best for them not to come. Your grandpa shows no recognition of anyone at all. He hasn't almost from the first day he came here. Alzheimer's is a terrible disease. I know you all love him and I'm sure he must have felt your love when he was well. Here is his room. If I can be of help, please call me and I'll come back and talk with you."

Ernie again hesitated, watching the nurse walk away. It was almost like he was being sent to a world of his own, where he would know no one. Even a feeling of emptiness came over Ernie. Slowly opening the door, he looked over at the bed and gasped as he saw his grandpa lying there.

"This is not grandpa. Please tell me, Lord, that I have the wrong room."

Closing the door behind him, he almost opened it again to walk away. Something moved him, pushing him toward the bed. Bending down to kiss the now emaciated forehead of his grandpa, great sobs came up from his throat. Tears rolled down his cheeks and he reached out to grasp the bony hand.

Suddenly, he felt a squeeze on his hand. Grandpa's eyes opened and he smiled.

"Ernie! I was just thinking of you and wondering when you would be coming to see me. You know, you've been away far too long. Come and sit here beside me and let's talk about you."

Ernie was shocked! He pulled a chair close to the side of the bed and thought, "What is this? Everyone said he wouldn't know me and here he is talking to me as he always did. What's going on here?"

"Well, Grandson. I hear you've made quite a name for yourself. I always knew you would be a great success. Ernie, your grandma and me loved you almost as much as we did your dad. I'll always remember those wonderful summers you came to see us. We would meet you at the bus station and take you home on the streetcar. Grandma would have all your favorite foods ready, and my goodness, how she loved to fix you desserts!"

"Grandpa," Ernie was now crying. "I'm sorry I've been away for so long. No job is worth being away from your loved ones. I wish I could go back and change things but I suppose it's too late."

"Why are you crying, Ernie? I'm the one who is happy to see you and you are right; we sometimes take the desire for money too seriously and forget the other things. Well, it's good to see you. You know, I'm going home. I suspect it will be any time now so let's talk awhile before I go."

Ernie, wanting to please his grandpa and still stunned by the conversation, said he was glad grandpa was going home and it would be wonderful.

"Do you remember the time we went blackberry picking and a lady came walking around the hill and we hid from her? She owned the land and I wasn't sure she wanted us to be there picking her berries. I guess I didn't teach you a very good lesson there, did I? I don't remember if we got many berries or not, but we had lots of fun. And your grandma covered you with sulphur to keep the chiggers away from you. And on the way home, we stopped by the creek and went swimming to wash the sulphur off.

Then there was the time we went fishing and caught a lot of small fish; I've forgotten what they were. We took them home to grandma and she got upset with us because they were too small to clean. What did we do with them? One other time we went fishing that I remember about. We were sitting on the creek bank when I heard someone coming by. I said we should hide because we had no license. I guess I didn't teach you a very good lesson then either.

My, we had a lot of fun, didn't we? Do you remember trying to skip rocks down by the pond? You were all upset because you couldn't get them to skip and cried all the way home. I think grandma promised you a butterscotch pie and I had to go to the store to get eggs. You wanted to go with me so we walked to the corner market and on the way home, a rainstorm came up and we got all wet."

Grandpa squeezed harder on Ernie's hand, and had a long, deep coughing spell.

"Those were good days, Ernie. We'll never get to live them again except in memory. Now you've grown into a fine young man and I'm so very proud of you."

Another coughing spell brought up some blood. Ernie was alarmed and wanted to call the nurse but grandpa assured him he was fine.

"Ernie, I know you've only been here a short time but I believe it best you go now. It was good to see you. You know, it was a miracle of God's that He let you come to me when I needed to see you. Go along now. Tell grandma I'm going home and I look forward to seeing her. Say hi to your dad. Go on now. Best you hurry."

Ernie, still in shock over what was happening, did as grandpa wished. He squeezed his hand, kissed him again on the forehead, and walked to the door without looking back or saying a word.

As he reached the door, he heard his grandpa say, "Mother, look at those beautiful clouds. I feel like I'm floating on them, and over there, look, it's McGlone Creek, and there is my old home on the Creek. The clouds are so soft………"   His voice faded away to nothing.

As Ernie passed the nurse's station, he looked at her, shrugged, and walked out the door without speaking.

Perhaps it was thirty minutes before he drove up to his grandma's apartment. As he walked into her living room, his dad was there and he and grandma were crying.

His dad got up, took Ernie by the hand and said, "We just received word that grandpa died. The nurse said she found him about five minutes after you left. She went to his room to check on him, saw he had a smile on his face, and then he just quit breathing."

For minute Ernie seemed deep in thought.

"You know, Dad.Something strange happened to me there at the nursing home. Grandpa talked with me about the good times we once had and then he told me he was going home. I thought he was talking about coming home, here, to where he and grandma live. But you know, Dad, he was talking about ……going home. I thought he was meandering in his thoughts but he meant it. I think he knew he was going home…to God!"

Tom McGlone

POSTSCRIPT

My days on the Creek are over. As I begin the drive away from the valley, I stop once more, get out of my car, and take one more stroll up the hillside. The warm yellow rays of the sun spread themselves across the heaven of eternity. The great ball itself is slowly sinking into a bed of deepening gray clouds, disappearing as though eaten by a monster shark. The rays gradually disappear and the thunder begins to roll across the valley and lightning streaks in the clouds now creating semi-darkness over the entire land.

Rain? Maybe! I sit there on the outcropping of limestone watching as nature displays its power over the Universe. It is only mid-afternoon and still the dimness of the day creates a desire to flee to shelter, or, to watch as this new creation take over the land below and the sky above. No longer do the birds sing, only an occasional chirp as though they are nesting for the night. Even a frog in the little stream nearby begins its chant. Quietness in the valley!

Life begins for each of us, and life ends for each of us. Joy and sadness mingle along the way. The Creek can be anywhere— it can be in some far off land, or, just over the ridge.

It can be with you in memory-in a nursing home-a hospital-a mansion-a country home, or sitting on a hillside It can be carried with you in your heart. Just close your eyes, remember it, and let your heart and soul be content. We all want to go back to our early home-this is what UP ON THE CREEK tries to inspire.

God creates. He also takes away. But He is there and gives us so much!

And we all have to say goodbyes to grandmas and grandpas, mas and pas, to life on the Creek. But the memories...ah, the memories...

Listen to the sighing of the pine boughs. What are they whispering? The oaks, the beeches, and the maples…….all have a story to tell……….if we would only hear.

Now it is time to go. I rise, walk back down the hillside. I muse at the land, its beauty, and God's creation. Only now, after time has aged and honed my vision could I really see it. . Only now were the memories of my life on the Creek etched into my mind, my heart and soul.

ABOUT THE AUTHOR

The author is a graduate of Miami University of Ohio, and spent most of his adult life around Suburbia Detroit. Since retiring, he and his wife, Joan, divide their time between Oscoda, Michigan and Berea, Kentucky.

Some of his early years were spent on the Creek which his Great, Great, Great, Grandfather Owen, settled in the year eighteen hundred. Tom recalls many of the stories, both fact and fiction, passed down by his ancestors.

Grandpa Tom Perry, a Civil War veteran, left a legacy for his many descendents and these stories serve to keep memories alive. Tom wants people to appreciate there is more to life than the hustle and bustle of the big cities and offers these stories to help folks relieve some of the stress of everyday living. Modern culture tends to make us forget the 'old days' and Tom tries to help us remember through his book—UP ON THE CREEK.